The Space Farmer

Lyle Garford

Dedication

This one is for Ryan and Mike

Published by:
Lyle Garford
Vancouver, Canada
Contact: lyle@lylegarford.com

ISBN 978-1-7772783-7-3

Cover photo Blue Planet Studio /Shutterstock.com

Book Design by Lyle Garford
www.lylegarford.com

First Edition 2022
Print Edition available on Amazon and other retailers.

Chapter One

Harlan rubbed his tired eyes for the fifth time in the last hour, knowing this was a sign he was losing focus. Despite that he was far too puzzled and on edge at the same time. He also wasn't ready to quit despite the doubts gnawing at his insides. But every time his inner cynic dismissed what he was seeing as just another false lead, the spark of hope alight in his soul at the thought this could be the real thing refused to disappear.

But figuring out whether he really had found something was the challenge.

He pulled out his mobile phone to check the time and groaned aloud at what he saw on the display. Now a bare few minutes away from midnight, the streetlights and signs on the nearby shops in the area around the rental apartment building he called home were already on. His alarm would go off far too early in the morning and it already felt like a long, tiring week at the office. But the light pollution from the city around him made the job of his telescope that much harder and he needed as many of the city lights as possible around him off. Fortunately, the property manager of the apartment building he lived in was generous enough to give him access to the building's roof three floors up from the ground to indulge his hobby.

With a sigh, he decided to try once more to find what he was looking for. This was the second night in a row he was up late engaging in the same search. The night before he was too tired and, being certain he would discover some sort of painfully obvious error was the cause, he dismissed what he found and put it aside for the next night. He fully expected to find whatever was wrong with what he did would now be clear. In his years working as a programmer, he learned one lesson many times, over and over again. If debugging needed to be done, fresh eyes and a clear mind were always good to have.

He looked at his notes one final time and made certain he was entering the right coordinates to the tablet computer he was using to guide his telescope to the right spot. After checking it twice, he sighed and crossed his fingers in hope this time he would succeed. With the most expensive eyepiece he owned attached, he knew this was his best shot at solving the small mystery now nagging at him so much that sleep this night would be hard to find if he didn't succeed. Carefully grasping the eyepiece, he once again peered into the depth of night sky above in search of an answer.

And, as before, the answer eluded him.

"Gahhh!" he said to himself in frustration, tearing himself away from the telescope and running his hand through his hair. "I don't bloody get this."

Harlan felt certain something anomalous was up there in a geostationary orbit. But in reality, certainty was proving impossible to find. When he focused on the coordinates and stared into the darkness to find it, what he got was simply more of the same mystery. Each time he looked, his brain registered what seemed an infinitesimally tiny wobble, which within a millisecond resolved into simply more of the emptiness of space.

And paradoxically, this made both perfect sense and seemed utterly nonsensical at the same time.

Harlan stood staring at the telescope, his shoulders slumped in frustration. After a moment of indecision he began packing up his equipment to head back downstairs to his apartment. He shook his head as he thought about what to do next.

"God, why do I do this to myself? I should take up knitting or something," he muttered, for he knew a hard choice was coming. But his mind strayed back to how he reached this point, failing to see what else he could have done to figure out what was happening.

Most of the people he knew enjoyed some sort of hobby to occupy their time when not drudging away at whatever job they had drifted into in life. While more than a few of his friends dabbled with diversions linking to scientific endeavours, specifically searching for extra-terrestrial life wasn't a hobby he shared with anyone else. Of course, he knew a broad spectrum of people in the world beyond his circle of friends were engaged in the same search as he was, but after a few hesitant attempts to connect with them he decided to keep his distance. Some of the serious science geeks out on the fringe could be downright weird.

Harlan acknowledged an objective observer might easily think of him as yet another member of that fringe element. As an unmarried single male, a few months shy of thirty years old, he was already uncomfortably close to the stereotype his friends readily assured him he was fitting. True, he had the luxury of a stable job as a computer programmer with a software company, although he was seriously underpaid. He would have moved on or tried to set up his own company long ago, but the boundless ambition he felt ten years ago somehow disappeared when contemplating at the thought of losing a steady paycheque and job benefits.

He'd had girlfriends along the way, but none of them stuck with him. They either revealed their true, high maintenance selves soon enough or decided someone who seemed to be an introverted science geek, spending most of his time staring at a computer screen, wasn't for them. That his spare time was spent searching for aliens didn't help. When the women he met learned of his hobby, their faces usually struggled to hide varying degrees of wary disbelief and dismay. Most simply rolled their eyes and took their attention elsewhere.

He couldn't help it, though. The possibility of alien life existing somewhere beyond the known limits of the planet humans call home was so alluring he couldn't let it go. He'd grown up devouring stories of early explorers sailing into the unknown and it was no stretch to see the spirit of those people was alive and well in the space program. While no one ever admitted it, he knew it was a given everyone attached to the space program secretly harboured a fervent hope they would have the thrill of making humanity's first contact with alien beings. Harlan was no exception, convincing himself it was actually little different than winning a lottery with really bad odds. But sooner or later, he was certain someone would win.

The hard reality of putting food on the table and paying the bills forced those young dreams to take a back seat as he grew older, for his family wasn't rich. His other problem was while his marks in school were good, those of others were excellent. So his only option was to finish school and focus on the day-to-day, mundane needs of building a life. But he was in the grip of the mystery of whether alien life existed and, as soon as he could, he began occupying his spare time with the search.

With the limited resources at his disposal, he quickly turned to focusing on the efforts of others. The Search For Extra-terrestrial Intelligence or SETI was a longstanding area of interest to scientists everywhere, but in recent years the efforts began to grow exponentially. Early work involved large telescopes like the Arecibo dish in Puerto Rico, but the amount of time available to spend specifically on SETI searches was restricted due to competition from other scientific projects. As such, the data gathered was limited in scope and volume.

This changed with the installation of a large telescope array in the California mountains almost twenty years ago. As the array was using new technology and was dedicated solely to SETI work, what used to be a relatively manageable trickle of SETI search information soon became a massive flood. The SETI scientists resorted to software to sort the most promising bits of information for detailed review. And all of it was made publicly available to the worldwide ranks of amateur SETI fans like Harlan.

Reasoning that even the best scientists could

overlook important information at times, Harlan decided to see if he could find something they somehow failed to notice or something they were seeing and totally misunderstood. He spent several evenings designing his own program to sift through the masses of data he downloaded from the SETI site and began running tests, focusing on searching for tiny anomalies that otherwise could be missed. Although any hint of success eluded him, he continued to make modifications. With the ability to work its way through data provided on its own, the program gave him free time to do other tasks.

But now, the reason he was up on the roof two nights in a row was that the program finally produced a result. After working its way through the data fed to it for several weeks, Harlan was stunned to find an automatic report from his program waiting for him when he woke one morning. The irony was he ended up cursing himself for having slept in on this of all mornings. With no time to review it, he was forced to rush off to work. He shouldn't have bothered, for his mind kept drifting to what was waiting for him at home. The day ended being one of his less productive efforts for the company.

The second he walked into his apartment after work that evening he made straight for his computer to dive into the details of what the program found for him. Within a few minutes he digested the gist of what the report covered and he frowned in response.

"Wow. That can't be," he said, muttering to himself. "It's ridiculous."

Pulling up the original source file he pinpointed the specific section which revealed the tiny anomaly his program found, a miniscule oddity in the data so small he was amazed to have picked it up. Harlan rubbed his face in confusion, for if this was a flaw it was beyond belief it could be there. After all, the SETI instruments were simply doing their job of recording what they found. And if it wasn't a flaw, the only possible conclusion was something was in fact there to produce the strange data.

His immediate reaction was to suspect it was a tiny bit of space junk causing the reading. But even as the thought came he dismissed it. The problem was things like satellites or even various bits of tiny space junk out there appeared very different in the SETI data, which was annotated automatically by the advanced software programs the researchers used to flag such elements. The SETI people knew exactly where each bit of junk was, regardless of size.

Still working on the assumption a problem was buried in the source data, he soon downloaded a fresh copy and compared it to the one his program generated the result from. He shook his head as he realized the outcome was the same. After puzzling over it without success he put it all away and went to fix himself dinner, but the mystery was still there when he picked it up again to look at it with fresh eyes. He knew he had no choice but to stay up late and turn his gaze to the stars, for he wouldn't sleep if he didn't.

On one hand the anomalous data seemed to indicate something was in a geostationary orbit over the earth. But it was so unusual the data could equally be a simple, strange glitch of some sort. He was fully expecting to find nothing as he pointed his telescope to the sky that first night and was thus stunned to find the ever so tiny wobble each and every time he looked at the coordinates the SETI data produced for him.

And this was why after two nights of staring at the same thing and considering every possible reason for what he was seeing, it remained paradoxical the data would lead him to something which made no sense whatsoever. Logic told him there must be some sense to it, however bizarre it may be. Harlan always subscribed to the notion the law of cause and effect was a universal principle, and that there was indeed order to the universe. In his world, if the reason for something happening wasn't clear, it was because we were suffering from an imperfect understanding of the universe and how it worked.

But now, after two nights staring at the same strange phenomenon with no resolution, Harlan's mind was wrestling with his new problem as he made his way back down to his ground floor apartment with his equipment. Despite the late hour and how early he knew his alarm would go off, he put his gear away and sat at his desktop computer. Pulling up his email program, he hesitated for a long minute before creating a new message file to send. With his fingers hovering over the keyboard he hesitated once again, before finally slumping back into his chair with a groan.

"God, do I need to do this?" he muttered to

himself.

He sat in front of his computer with the blank email on his screen for almost a full ten minutes considering the problem thoroughly. The angst he was feeling over what he was thinking of doing was real, for he would be exposing himself to a very tough audience. The opinion of one person in particular he didn't want to disappoint weighed on him. After going over every possibility in his mind, it remained all too likely he was missing some mundane element that his audience would find and the ensuing ridicule he'd endure wasn't a pleasant prospect. But the tiny, inner flare of hope which kept him glued to the spot was the thought he was on the cusp of beating the dismal odds against him. Finding something everyone else was missing was too great a prize to ignore.

And maybe, just maybe, that something was alien.

Harlan sighed, for he knew he needed a reality check and a discussion with the others about this. Having made his decision he began typing with ever increasing speed. If he sent the email, he knew he would get what he was looking for one way or another. The words flowed almost without effort onto his computer screen, for the possibilities were boundless and inspiration seized him.

What if, he asked himself as he typed, this was indeed an alien craft hiding in plain sight? Maybe it was employing some kind of technology like the military used to hide from enemy radar? It would need to be very, very good in order to elude the prying eyes of various militaries around the world, and who knew, this could even be some sort of advanced satellite. But if it was an alien ship, what was it doing in a geostationary orbit?

Harlan included the detailed coordinates of the anomaly in his email, making certain the people reading his message would know exactly where and how close the object was. The thought it was beyond belief no one found the anomaly before this kept nagging at him, but each time it surfaced so did the same notion that even in lotteries with the absolute worst odds, someone was going to win.

Several minutes later the flood of words finally slowed to a trickle and he finished his message. After reading it through twice and making a few small corrections he was satisfied with the result, but he couldn't bring himself to hit send. Feeling the angst well up again, he sat back in his chair trying to decide how he felt about it. The thought came that the torment he was feeling was a measure of how truly important it was to him that what he found was the real thing. If the outcome was the opposite, he knew his spirits would be crushed, although that was nothing new. He shook his head, realizing everything he was thinking probably meant he was fitting the profile of nerd science geek far more than he wanted to admit.

His moved his hand toward the computer keypad to hit send two more times, but pulled it back in indecision each time. He rubbed his chin and sighed in frustration over what to do, searching for an answer that wouldn't come. The late hour and his tiredness didn't help. And neither did the large bulk of Spock landing on the desk beside him with a thud.

"Shit!" said Harlan, his concentration jarred in momentary surprise, before he realized who it was.

"Maaoorrw!" said the big orange and white tabby cat in response, staring back at Harlan.

Harlan sighed as he reached out to scratch behind the cat's ear.

"Don't do that, Spock. You scared the crap out of me."

But Harlan knew he shouldn't have been surprised. Living on the ground floor in his apartment building meant he could enjoy a small patio deck outside his suite like Spock's owner, his next-door neighbour Isaac. With the pleasant early summer weather they were enjoying Harlan got to know the old man and his cat who earlier in the spring moved into the suite next door, having good conversations together when they were both outside in the evening. Harlan usually left his patio door open in summer evenings, giving free reign as a result for Spock to visit in search of the kitty treats the cat knew Harlan would have for him.

"Sorry, Spock," said Harlan, stroking the cat absentmindedly and staring back at the computer screen. "My mind is on other things."

The cat seemed to sense it. Strolling across the desk with his tail in the air to stand in front of Harlan, the cat turned and stared at the screen for several long moments as if reading the email for himself. Harlan could only laugh as all he could now see in his line of sight was Spock's raised tail and ass.

"All right, Spock, I probably deserve that. Now

get out of the way...no, don't do that, for God's sake!"

Spock was stepping forward unexpectedly onto the keyboard, shuffling back and forth a bit in search of a prime spot, before promptly flopping down on it as if it were the most comfortable bed anywhere. Harlan groaned and picked him up, moving him back off to the side. Stroking the now aggrieved looking cat for a few moments to placate him, Harlan turned back to the computer screen to focus once again on his task. His jaw fell open as he did, for the draft email was no longer on the screen. Quickly checking his sent mail, he confirmed it was indeed already in the inboxes of all of his friends. Somehow, Spock seemed to have made his decision for him.

"Oh, damn..." said Harlan, turning to glare at the cat.

Spock was now sitting there licking a paw as if nothing was happening, but seeing Harlan watching him he stopped.

"Meoww!" said Spock once again.

Harlan knew that if a cat could smirk, the expression now on Spock's face was what it would look like. And Harlan also knew exactly what was being expected of him.

Harlan sighed. "Come on then, you silly beast. Let's get you a treat."

***

Fridays were usually Harlan's favourite day of the week. Although his work as a programmer paid the bills and some jobs held greater challenges than others, the same routine elements of the work were long since beginning to wear on him. The thought of a career change crossed his mind on more than one occasion, but the question was what to change to. Even worse to consider was whether he wanted to pay the price for doing so.

As a result, Fridays were the day Harlan felt like a flower coming into an ever so brief bloom that would last the weekend. But the other problem with his job were demanding clients that changed their minds about what they wanted as often as they put on new clothes.

While normally he could muster more patience, today was particularly difficult as he tried to meet the needs of one of the most finicky clients of the company. If it weren't for the fact he knew the two business owners he was dealing with were highly educated professionals, he would have sworn they both had the brains of a gnat. In reality they were actually nice people, which made his job all the more challenging, but the importance of freezing the design when working to create something new was a critical need to understand, especially if they wanted to stay on budget.

As Harlan finally walked out the door of the office in relief his phone pinged with an incoming text. He glanced at the time before he checked the message, groaning to himself on finding it was already almost an hour past when he was supposed to be free of the clutches of his employer. He was thus unsurprised to see the text was a brief query as to where he was. This time he sighed and stopped a moment to send a quick reply he was on the way. No responses came in since the email was sent two nights before, but that was exactly what he was expecting. He would learn soon enough what the recipients of his message thought.

The Lamplighter Diner was several blocks away in a much older and rather seedier part of town, away from the business district. Affectionately known as The Lamp by his friends and everyone else that congregated there, it was a combination diner, pub, and music venue serving anything it could to make a buck. Although out of the way, The Lamp survived by having good, cheap food and, even better, an array of decent, cheap beer on offer.

Harlan knew the usual crowd of his friends would already be there, for the unspoken agreement was no matter what was going on in their lives, Friday nights were for hanging out at The Lamp. Occasionally a musician or two would appear later in the evenings to help The Lamp sell more beer. They all stumbled home from The Lamp well past midnight on more than one occasion as a result.

Normally Harlan looked forward to heading for The Lamp as a place to decompress to start his weekend, but he remained on edge and preoccupied as he made his way down the street to meet his fate. Because of that he failed to notice a van pull away from where it was parked outside his office and begin following him slowly down the street, stopping and slipping back into a parking spot periodically to ensure it didn't overtake him as he went. The van was black and didn't stand out in any way, except for the small array of strange looking antennas on the roof and the slightly darkened, tinted glass of its windows which made it hard to see inside.

And it followed him all the way to The Lamp.

Chapter Two

"Listen love, so what do you say we ditch this lot and find somewhere for just the two of us, huh?"

The speaker had a slight Caribbean accent and was a black male with light, coffee coloured skin and a thick fringe of curly dark hair on top of his head, although the sides and back were shaved close to his head. Like the woman he was talking to, both were well into their late twenties. She knew he was trying to ply her with his most winning look, but she chose to ignore him and continue to stare at the screen of her phone. But she also knew he wasn't giving up that easily.

"Keiko. It's only because I love you. You know that."

"God," said Keiko, rolling her eyes without taking them off the screen of her phone. "Please shut up, Jordi."

The two nearest people beside them at the table looked up from their own phones and laughed. Jordi glared at both of them before turning back to Keiko one more time.

"The truth is you want him and not me, isn't it? That's why you sent Harlan a text to see where he is, because you can't wait to drape yourself all over him and make some babies. You're in love with him, aren't you? What does he have I don't?"

Keiko groaned as the two people laughed even harder and she glowered at Jordi from the corner of her eye. On hearing the laughter the rest of the people sitting at the table pulled their gaze away from their own phones to listen in.

"He doesn't have anything over you, because you're both a pair of total dweebs," replied Keiko, trying to add as much disdain to her voice as she could. "And I'm not interested because anything you two might spawn would likely have three heads. Find someone else to breed mutations with, why don't you?"

"Damn, hope springs eternal, eh, Jordi?" said one of the other males at the table, grinning as he took a sip of his beer. "Maybe I should try since you and Harlan are striking out."

"Good luck with that, Spider. Just don't put money on it working," said Keiko, as Jordi groaned beside her.

"Hmm. I think she's already decided she doesn't want any Mexican mutations either, Spider," said the woman sitting across the table from him.

The man called Spider laughed. "Yes, yes, I know. I was just seeing if she's changed her mind. Keiko's a hot babe and someone has to keep her happy. I know, it won't be me. If I was Jose Mendez, the rich and talented engineer like I wanted to be, I'll bet she'd be thinking differently. But I'm just 'Spider' Mendez, a poor and struggling science fiction writer working at a menial job. I'm not competition, Jordi."

"We love you all, but none of you are competition," said the same woman. "Keiko has high standards and so do the rest of us."

That generated a snort of laughter from another male listening to the banter.

"The standards must have changed somewhere along the way," he said, toying with the now almost empty pint glass in his hand. "What standards were you using when it came to Robert, Keiko?"

Keiko sighed and shook her head as she thought about a response, not taking her eyes off her phone for a long moment before finally putting it down to look around the table at the people watching her.

"You know, it's only because I love you all, although God knows why, that I'm going to answer that. Robert was a mistake. It took me time to realize this. I've even confessed that to my parents, who certainly told me on more than one occasion I should just go find myself a nice young man of Japanese descent like me. Everyone is entitled to a mistake and we all know the rest of you have spent time in bed with your share of mistakes, so don't sit there feeling smug. And now that I fully understand my body has its own asshole and I don't need to be sleeping beside a second one, life is much better. So you are right, Clifford, the standards are now thankfully higher."

"But aren't we all at least likeable assholes, Keiko?" said Spider.

"Somewhat likeable. And that doesn't get you very far," replied Keiko, her head already buried back in her phone.

Everyone laughed again and the woman sitting beside her raised her glass in toast.

"To high standards."

They all touched glasses and echoed the toast before turning back to stare at their phones once more. Keiko found she was too tired and couldn't refocus back on the article she was reading moments before, so she scrolled absently through a popular social media app. But despite her best efforts, her mind strayed back to the question Clifford brought up. Although the relationship ended several months ago, the split still seemed raw. She couldn't blame any of her friends for thinking what they did over it all, for with the perfection of hindsight it was clear they were right.

She sighed to herself, realizing how easy it was to take her friends for granted. She wasn't kidding when she said she loved them all, although what wasn't said was that they all drove her crazy to varying degrees. In more lucid moments she acknowledged they likely felt the same way about her. She looked around the table, contemplating each of them in turn, and smiled to herself at how diverse they were. They all knew each other from their high school days and everyone seemed to enjoy the diversity of their group of friends. Getting together was never dull.

She knew it was unusual they were all still close friends despite all having graduated a little over ten years ago now. They all went on separate paths as they pursued different education and careers, but none of them strayed far and ultimately they all remained living in the same city. Even more uncommon, each of them made a point of maintaining contact with the others in the group. Somehow they even managed to find homes all in the same general area within walking distance of The Lamp.

The appeal of The Lamp was hard to resist. Originally a warehouse built of burnt orange bricks well over a hundred and twenty years before, it evolved several decades earlier into its current incarnation as a diner and tavern. The name came from the use of gas lamps to light the streets in the area around it, although their usage was dwindling by the time the warehouse was built.

By the prohibition era the building was converted to its current use, but electric light was predominant by then. Garish neon signs everywhere did even more to light the streets and The Lamp was no exception, needing a beacon to compete for patrons. When the current owners were asked about the murky history of The Lamp, their story always included the real possibility of it serving as a speakeasy for a time.

While The Lamp may have seen better days and the decor was decidedly tired, it was a favourite among younger people in the area. For the first few years after graduating high school it certainly was theirs for a time. The rustic brick walls with scuffed and well-worn wood floors lent a unique, unpretentious atmosphere to the place. Good, inexpensive food and cheap beer went a long way to making up for deficiencies. As regular patrons of The Lamp on Friday nights, their server Carrie made sure their favourite large table was always set aside for them. That was good, for on Friday nights The Lamp was usually packed with young people. With a view out a nearby large window of all manner of people walking by on the street the table was a prime location.

That they were all making a point of meeting for drinks and dinner on Friday nights was something that developed over time. It wasn't always this way, for they all made connections with other people as they built their young lives. But the key was they all stayed connected with each other over the years and at this stage in their lives, they all seemed to have found themselves more or less in the same space. None were married and all of them struggled with relationships that came and went, never seeming to work.

The unspoken, collective agreement they did have was an acknowledgment that while they were obviously all good enough to get decent marks in school, none of them had ever been the star pupils they wanted to be. With the shared common experience of having their young dreams begin to fade and the fact they were all living nearby, none of them seemed surprised as one by one they gravitated back to their favourite watering hole. The attendance varied from week to week, but all of them made a point of being there to check in as long as no other pressing engagements were at hand.

Although she dismissed him easily, the black male named Jordi actually had a very different background, starting with a British father whose sense of humour led him to name his son as he did. Being an actual Geordie from Newcastle in England, it made sense to the father. But Jordi himself was born on the Caribbean island of Antigua, where his mother was from, and he spent his childhood there before moving to North America just as he entered his teen years.

Jordi was a programmer working at the same company as both Harlan and Keiko, which meant she saw both of them far more than she really wanted to. In truth they were all good friends, but the two men were also both major nerds in their own ways. Because they were all seriously underpaid, Jordi turned loose his inner penchant for finding new ways to make up for that fact. He was tight lipped about his current project, which seemed to involve some sort of online business running out of his home island of Antigua. He was tall and lanky, and certainly handsome enough in his own way. A nice guy at heart, but she felt no attraction to him.

Jose Mendez, or Spider as he preferred to be called, was even more of a nerd than Harlan and Jordi combined. Keiko wouldn't have thought it possible, but no one would argue the point if she made it. After starting on a science degree while dreaming of a career in engineering, the reality of his marks brought a rude awakening. Dropping out to rethink his plans led to finding a job to pay to the bills while he did that. Like the others, it became far too easy to enjoy the steady paycheque from working as a call centre agent handling insurance claims.

Claiming his real goal in life was to be an author, Spider spent all of his spare time writing science fiction books. When asked where the nickname Spider came from all he would do is grin and say the hint was he liked puns and hybrid fantasy science fiction. His query letters to agents and publishers generated a stack of rejections in response over the years, when they bothered to respond at all.

Undeterred, he dove into self-publishing and was

now at a point where he was making money. He wasn't getting rich, but he made enough to pay his costs with a little profit on the side. While Spider undoubtedly knew the odds of ever gaining a meaningful measure of worldwide success were slim, Keiko was also certain the fire was still burning inside him to make it happen.

Keiko was pulled out of her reverie as she sensed the woman sitting beside her stir. Keiko knew others considered her good looking, but Nyota was a rival. She was black like Jordi, but her dark hair softly curled down past her shoulders. As Keiko turned toward her she saw Nyota was staring at Clifford.

"Whatever it is, the answer is no, Clifford," said Nyota.

Clifford grunted and shook his head. "You haven't heard what I was going to say yet."

"I don't need to, but you are going to ask the question whether I want to hear it or not."

"Of course. Thing is, you think I'm going to spout some weird stuff about aliens and their deal with the cabal ruling the world which keeps us serfs under their thumb, but I was just going to ask how your week was. I'm tired of staring at my phone, unlike everyone else at this table. Getting hungry too. I am hoping Harlan gets here before I drink myself under the table."

"My week sucked, thank you for asking, although I'd rather not think about it a second longer than I have to. Hopefully the pinnacle of my career will someday be more than assistant manager of a steak house that's trying to be a great destination, but failing miserably. Apparently I should have set my sights higher if all a degree in Economics gets you is sore feet and a lot of customers interested in no more than staring at my boobs."

"Speaking as a connoisseur of female anatomy, I'd say your customers obviously have discriminating taste. But seriously, you could always go back and get a second degree. I'd suggest Science, but all that got me was a totally boring job doing quality control on a soft drink production line. Same shit every day."

"Listen, I'm already surrounded by a crowd of science geeks getting used and abused like me. I've been surrounded all my life by science geeks. My parents both were. Haven't you ever wondered why I'm named Nyota? Don't know why I need to waste time and money getting a science degree just so I can join you all moaning about the same thing. But I thought you said they were talking about moving you into management?"

Clifford laughed. "That didn't last long. They suggested I should consider being a management trainee. Funny how being a management trainee would end up paying me less than I make right now. Oh, the sky is the limit they tell me, assuming my performance warrants raising me to their lofty heights. Problem was my finely honed bullshit meter got me in trouble. Apparently expressing concern about a reduction in pay was the wrong answer. Could be I got a little cynical in my response when they asked what I thought about the company mission statement too. Of course, the other person in line for the spot happened to have a splendid set of tits. Just like you, in fact. It was just window dressing that I got interviewed at all."

"Good thing you didn't tell them about the aliens or how you think the earth is flat. They'd have you sweeping floors and taking the trash out," said the other remaining woman at the table, toying with her glass of white wine.

As Keiko turned to look at her she saw Deanna was wearing another of what she thought of as vintage sixties hippie girl dresses. Despite standing out like a unicorn in a field of cattle, the look suited her. Deanna's long, straight brown hair and a pleasing face suited her clothes.

"Well, I can't let them know I'm on to them, can I?" said Clifford. "You wait, one day I'll get the goods and expose the cabal for what it is. And how was your week, my dear, lovely Deanna?"

"Probably better than the rest of you and thanks for asking, you crazy flatterer. Hey, I like my job. I may never get rich as a social worker helping old people, but the rewards are more than money. Thing is, if all of you have enjoyed a tough week you should be on the lookout for more. Mercury has gone into retrograde and is going to be there a while. It could get more than a little weird out there."

"And what in God's name does that mean?" asked Spider.

"It means there can be turbulence and disruption encompassing a whole host of things. Communication, relationships, you name it. Crazy stuff can happen when this planet is in retrograde."

"You do realize your science nerd friends think

astrology and all that other spiritual mumbo jumbo you believe in is just a load of horse crap, right?" said Jordi, finally looking up from his phone to join the conversation.

"Of course. Not everyone is attuned to the higher planes and you would think that if you weren't. But I predict a day will come when you will all understand there is more to all of this than just the material world around us."

"Will drinking more beer help me reach enlightenment?" said Spider, flagging down their server. "I sure hope so, because my glass is empty."

Their regular server steered a path over to their table and smiled as she came to take their orders.

"Might as well celebrate getting rejected yet again. I'll have another too, Carrie," said Jordi, staring at Keiko as he spoke.

"Anyone ready to order yet?" said the server.

"We're still waiting for Harlan, Carrie," said Nyota. "But if he doesn't get here in the next five minutes I'll order. I'm starving."

"Starved for love, too, I'll bet. I could help with that," said Jordi.

"Don't think she's that desperate, Jordi," said Clifford, before turning to look around the table. "Speaking of Harlan, you all read that email he sent, right? What do you think?"

Several people groaned aloud and turned back to stare at their phones.

"My first thought was the guy is obsessed," said Jordi. "I admire his perseverance, but I figure if you have to be obsessed about something you should make it worth your while. You know, on something that could make you pots full of money."

"Has it occurred to you there could be a reason I mentioned a while back you two are both total dweebs?" said Keiko. "Well, there is, and it's because you're both obsessed. He's focused on finding aliens while you're focused on dreaming up financial scams."

"Well, I for one am at least a little excited. I'll keep an open mind about what he has to say," said Clifford. "Who knows, this could be the big break that proves the aliens really are running the show in this world. It wasn't what I was expecting, but you have to be ready for the unexpected. Anything is possible."

"I wouldn't get your hopes up too much, Clifford," said Nyota. "Even just finding aliens would be a massive discovery. Getting proof they are running the planet is a whole other ballgame. Not that I believe any of this, you understand. And the likelihood he has managed to do that is basically zero."

"Well, I agree. I honestly figure the whole SETI research thing is a smokescreen set up to deflect attention away from the topic. They put on this veneer of scientific respectability, so when anybody asks they can show them empty hands and say sorry, haven't found anything yet. Nothing to see here, people. Move along. But hey, I'll listen to what he has to say. I'm big enough to admit there could be other explanations for something."

As he finished Clifford looked around the table for some support, but found none as their heads were all buried in their phones once again. The only response he got was from Jordi, who spoke without looking up from his phone's screen.

"Well, I have another explanation. You went off to see your doctor again and he prescribed some kind of funky stuff with extra special ingredients for you to take, I'll bet."

***

Harlan steeled himself as he reached The Lamp and walked in. He didn't bother looking around, for he already knew where everyone would be and he made his way directly to the table. As he did the van pulled up on the street outside and hesitated for a moment as a parking stall affording a perfect view of the entrance to The Lamp conveniently opened up directly across the street. Ignoring the vehicle behind it honking displeasure at having the lane blocked for too long, the van slipped into the now empty stall and parked.

"Thank God he's here," said Nyota. "We can order something to eat now."

"Sorry I'm late everyone. Had the clients from hell and couldn't get away."

"The Callahan account, right?" said Jordi.

"Got it the first time, Jordi," said Harlan.

"Better you than either of us, Harlan," said Keiko. "You are more patient than Jordi and I put together. I'd have murdered them by now."

"Carrie, can we order? We're starving," said Keiko.

Having seen Harlan come in their server was already on her way to the table, knowing they would want her soon enough. No one needed to look at the menus, for they knew them by heart. The only thing that varied was the daily fresh menu, scrawled on a large chalk board hanging on a nearby wall. After Carrie finished taking their orders and walked away everyone went back to staring at their phones, not noticing the man wearing sunglasses and a ball cap walk in the entrance and look around, letting his gaze settle on Harlan's table. They also never saw him stand there long enough for Carrie to finally go over and ask if he needed help, but he simply shook his head and left.

At the table Harlan looked warily about, knowing sooner or later someone would bring up the email. The wait wasn't long, as Clifford was the only one not staring deliberately at his phone. He was sitting across the table from Harlan, grinning as he toyed with his now half empty second pint of beer. Harlan raised an eyebrow to signal an invitation to get on with it, but Carrie showed up to drop off a beer for him. Clifford was still grinning as Harlan took a sip, turning his attention back to him.

"Nice weather we're having, huh?" said Clifford.

Harlan shook his head. "Asshole. Come on, spit it out."

Clifford's face took on a mocking, aggrieved look and he held up a hand in disbelief.

"What? I ask a simple question and get told I'm an asshole. I was merely acknowledging I know you've been staying up late looking at the stars again. Perfect weather for it, not a cloud in the sky."

"Yes. Yes, it is. Now please get on with it. You think I'm a lunatic, don't you?"

Clifford shrugged. "Maybe. I'm pretty sure everyone else here does, but me? I'm willing to keep an open mind. You might have found my aliens, after all. I hadn't expected them to be operating so openly this close to earth, but hey, anything is possible. So have they contacted you? Better be careful, if they figure out you've found them you might find yourself swimming with the fish permanently. Don't think they want to be found."

Harlan sighed and shook his head.

"Of course they haven't contacted me, Clifford. I only just found this in the data two days ago and I have no idea how they would know that. Right, what about the rest of you?"

Harlan looked around the table hoping for a response, but no one even acknowledged they heard him. He let his gaze finally rest on Keiko.

"So this is all the support I get? The only one willing to talk to me is our resident crazy person who believes in worldwide conspiracies?"

Harlan waited patiently, knowing she would relent sooner or later. Keiko finally sighed and put her phone down.

"What do you want me to say, Harlan? Should I lie and tell you how impressed I am, or should I just confirm Clifford isn't the only crazy person at this table?"

"I know it sounds ridiculous, but as I said in the email I have no explanation for this. It is a fact there is a weird blip in the SETI data. I can show it to any of you who care to not just dismiss me outright. And while you are at it you can come over and look through my telescope at it and see for yourself."

"A rather cunning ploy to get Keiko over to your place late at night," said Jordi. "And afterwards a nice glass of wine and great conversation about what it all means, right? Who knows where the evening could go?"

"Give it a rest, Jordi. I won't be at his place alone with him late at night any more than I would be at yours."

"Harlan?" said Deanna. "This may come as a surprise, but I am willing to keep an open mind too. I firmly believe there is much more to the universe than any of us realize, as I think you know. I was telling them all Mercury is in retrograde before you showed up and that means seriously weird stuff is totally possible to happen in periods like this. Having said that, I'll take your word for it about what you are seeing, but you have to admit it's pretty sketchy proof. Weird data in some spreadsheet? Maybe it's just a gremlin in the software. Your spot wobbles and disappears on you when you look at it? Could be a glitch with your telescope. Unless it's your eyeballs, because you've been smoking some really weird shit lately. In other words, you're going to have to do better than this, even for me."

"Yes," said Nyota. "Especially after the last time you thought you had something. We all spent a bunch of time helping you look at your glitch and even helped with composing your message to SETI. Remember how far that got you?"

"Okay, I admit that was a rookie screwup on my part," said Harlan. "At least the SETI people were good about it and let me down gently. But seriously, I think this time is different. I can't see any reasonable explanation for what I am seeing and, believe me, I've lost a lot of sleep the last few nights going over this. If I'm going to make another presentation to SETI, I really, really need a reality check. Can I at least get one of you to come over and look at this?"

As Harlan looked around the table he saw they were either back staring at their phones or suddenly finding something to look at in the bottom of their beer glass. He sighed and reached for his own glass, but Clifford finally spoke up.

"All right, Harlan. I'll come over and have a look, but it won't be till maybe later next week. I'm busy the rest of the weekend."

Harlan tried not to look disappointed, for it would mean yet more delay. He was firmly in the grasp of this puzzling anomaly and he wanted nothing more than to keep tearing at it until the mystery was solved.

"I tell you what, Harlan, I'll come over and have a look too," said Spider. "It'll have to be some night next week for me, too. Maybe Clifford and I can coordinate something. What the hell, if nothing else maybe it'll give me a new idea for a book."

"How's the latest one doing, Spider?" said Nyota.

"Not bad, but it'll take a while. When you are writing a series most people don't want to buy any of them unless they are all available. That way if they like the first book, they don't have to wait to read the rest of them."

"This is the one with a Latino hero as your hook,

isn't it?"

"It is. That might take a while to catch on too, but I'm optimistic. Hey, how many mainstream science fiction tv shows and movies have you ever seen with Latino characters, let alone one with the central character as the hero? I ask you. Systemic discrimination is what it is. But my time has come, I can feel it. I can make it happen."

"Well, at least someone around here still has enough optimism to think they can make their dreams happen" said Nyota, allowing a look of disappointment to cross her face. "I think mine fell by the wayside when I graduated from University."

"I've still got dreams," said Jordi, without looking up from his phone. "I'm going to make a shitload of money with my new project."

"You mean your latest scam," said Clifford.

"Call it what you will. You'll see when the time comes. At least I have something I'm looking forward to. It may not be what I originally thought I'd be doing in life, but making money is what it's all about and I'll pull it off."

"What about you, Keiko? What was your dream when you were younger?" asked Nyota.

"Not to be doing what I'm doing now."

"Right, so let's see if I have this straight," said Nyota. "There's me, going nowhere putting my expensive education to work as a bloody trainee in a restaurant. We have Clifford and Harlan, who both seem to have evolved to a point where their purpose in life is to find aliens. Might as well lump Spider in there too, since engineering didn't pan out. Not sure pinning hopes on finding aliens is a recipe for making that next great book happen, Spider. And I figure Keiko here is one of those people who never had a sense of what they wanted to do in life and still doesn't. Jordi is reduced to dreaming up scams, so that leaves you, Deanna. Are your dreams all shattered too?"

"Well, no. I like helping people, so I'm in the right place for me. As I said, I'll never get rich and I'm okay with that. I disagree with Jordi about the money thing. But my real dream is to grow my consciousness of the spiritual world around us. There's always room to grow."

"And drinking that glass of wine in your hand is going to help grow that consciousness, is it?" said Keiko. "You got something special added to it? Damn, maybe I should be drinking that instead of this beer."

Deanna shrugged. "Of course it's not helping. Quite the opposite, in fact. But we all came here as spirits to live and be in something magnificent. The universe has many blessings for us and that includes wine and beer. Used in moderation and in a positive way, they help to build connections with each other. The better we know each other, the more likely we are to be more compassionate and caring."

"So how come I'm not way more well connected than I am?" said Clifford. "Damn, I've poured enough beer down my throat in my time to float a ship. But why do you hang around with a bunch of losers like us, Deanna?"

Deanna let a look of weary tolerance appear on her face and was about to reply when Carrie appeared with an armload of food. Once their plates were in front of them Nyota raised her glass in toast.

"Well, we may all be losers but at least we provide company for each other. Cheers, everyone."

"You are only losers if you think you are," said Deanna. "Mistakes are how we learn and find our true purpose in life. I've made my share of mistakes, so I'm a loser like you all too. It just didn't require drinking an ocean of beer to figure that out. And for the record, I'm still here because I like all of you."

A silence descended as they all began to eat, remaining even as one by one they finished their meals. Harlan could see a few of them toying with their drinks, obviously weighing the notion of having another, but no one ordered more. Most of them looked tired and he surmised their week at work must have been as brutal as his. Clifford was the first to pay for his bill and leave. Clifford acknowledged the look of surprise Harlan was wearing on his face and grimaced in response.

"Yeah, I know, I'm usually the last to leave, but I'm bagged. I was trapped in endless meetings all day. If I stick around I'll just drink myself under the table and I've got a busy weekend ahead of me. See you all next week."

As he was walking toward the door Harlan called after him.

"Clifford, don't forget to call Spider. It would be great if you two could have a look at this soon."

Clifford stopped and looked startled for a moment before remembering and waving a hand in acknowledgment as he continued out the door. His departure started a slow exodus as others called for their tabs to pay. Keiko was still nursing her drink as Jordi eyed her while paying his bill.

"I'm heading for The Anchor on the other side of the harbour. They've got a few bands happening later tonight. Want to join me, Keiko?"

"Not tonight, thanks. It was a long week. I'm going home to soak in my tub. If I could soak my brain for an hour or so that would be even better."

"Are you sure? Come on, it'll be fun."

"Jordi, give it up. If my choices were to pick the lint off my sofa or go out with you, I'd chose dealing with the lint every time. I like you, I really do, but not enough to go out with you. Understand?"

Jordi was silent, glancing at Harlan for a moment, before hanging his head.

"Understood. Can't blame a guy for trying. See you all next week."

One by one the rest of them paid their bills and left. Harlan saw Keiko was about to call for hers too, but he caught her attention by reaching out to touch her hand.

"Stay for a bit? Please?"

Keiko stared at him for a moment and pulled her hand away, but she stayed where she was. Both Harlan and Keiko waved goodbye to the only other people left at the table as they rose to go and watched in silence as their friends walked out the door, leaving them alone together.

And once again, none of them made note of the van still parked across the street. They also failed to notice the camera with a large telephoto lens attached to it taking pictures from inside the van of each of them as they left.

Chapter Three

Harlan turned his attention back to Keiko, who was sitting across the table staring at him in silence. Carrie came by and looked at them with curiosity evident on her face, asking if they wanted more drinks. Harlan said yes at the same time as Keiko said no. This time Carrie raised an eyebrow.

Harlan sighed. "Split one more beer with me?"

Keiko relented and shrugged. "Sure, why not."

Once Carrie left to get their drink Harlan spoke. "Thank you for staying."

"When I figure out why I did, I'll let you know."

Harlan sighed once again. "Well, I'm hoping there is some kind of positive reason you did. You know, maybe even because you like me a little bit. I expect the fact I've found yet another reason for you to think I'm wacko doesn't help."

"You think?" said Keiko, rolling her eyes.

"Yes, I know. If I was to poll all the women in here tonight and ask them if searching for aliens as a hobby was a feature they might find attractive in a man, I figure the results wouldn't be giving me inspiration to carry on. But this really is me, Keiko. I'm not some secret axe murderer or a pyromaniac or anything like that. I'm just a regular guy with a slightly offbeat hobby. Other people keep bees or sing in barbershop quartets or do crocheting. I like to look at the stars and, in particular, I'd like to follow what the SETI people are doing. Does that make me so weird?"

"Well, it certainly makes you a serious nerd by pretty much everyone's standards, Harlan."

She was stopped from continuing as Carrie showed up with their drinks, already portioned out for them.

"Well, okay, but am I the kind of nerd you could maybe like?" said Harlan, after the server left.

Keiko rolled her eyes again. "Of course you are. But what you want to know is whether liking you means I want to jump into a relationship. Harlan, this may be hard to believe, but I have no idea."

Harlan toyed with his glass of beer and took sip.

"I guess I can believe it, although I'm not sure what it means for the future. Still wrestling with the breakup, huh?"

Keiko stayed silent for a long moment before finally replying.

"Harlan, I went out with him for almost six years of my life. I struggle with the fact it took me that long to realize how much of an asshole he is. I see now that I was probably attracted to his dominance. He always seemed so self-assured and confident. I, of course, have never had a clear idea of what I wanted to do in life or where I wanted to be. I probably attached myself to him because it seemed like a good idea at the time, to hang onto someone who was going places and I could live vicariously as a result. That and I wanted to party when I was younger. Shit, what do I know? Bottom line, here I am, pushing thirty years old, and I still feel like I'm drifting. I'm quite sure everyone thinks I'm high maintenance to boot. Who knows, maybe I am. Meanwhile, the only attention I'm getting is from a nerd looking for aliens and another nerd looking for get rich quick schemes. Hmm, not sure Deanna's planets are aligning for me. Maybe my rising sign planet is getting squished by my moon or a bloody comet or something."

Harlan laughed. "Maybe. Have to check with Deanna about that, because I wouldn't know. Look, all I know is I'm attracted to you. I have been for years. Maybe it's because our stars are crossed somehow, because I just never had what seemed like a real chance with you. I was too geeky in high school and you seemed to find everyone else far more interesting. But I'm still here, Keiko, and still interested. And I know I maybe have competition."

Keiko sighed and downed a big portion of her drink before finally speaking.

"I don't know what I want, Harlan. Jordi isn't competition, for the record. I like him as a person and I can socialize with him, but he is too much like Robert sometimes. No, make that more than just sometimes. You? I don't know, Harlan. I need some time and space to consider that. I do know you are a good man at heart, despite being the total nerd you clearly are. I just have to sort myself out inside."

"Okay. So it's fair to say you aren't dismissing the notion of you and me together out of hand?"

This time she remained silent a long time before responding, leaving Harlan feeling on edge for what the answer might be.

"Yes, Harlan. Against my better judgement, I am not dismissing this idea. But give me time, please. And I make absolutely no promises. Harlan, I don't want you following me around like a puppy dog. Prepare yourself for the possibility I might find someone else or just tell you to get lost."

"Fair enough, Keiko. I've already found a place for you in my heart. I'm going to do my best to wriggle my way into yours, one day at a time. And I promise to try and not be weird while I'm doing it."

Keiko smiled. "That would be a good start. And making me laugh is always good, too."

As she finished speaking she poured the rest of her beer into his glass.

"And now I'm going to leave you for the night, because I really am tired and am going home alone to soak in my tub. By the way, I trust you understand this doesn't mean I believe any of this nonsense about aliens, either."

Harlan sighed. "I know. Everyone thinks I am wasting my time and haven't found anything of consequence. Who knows? Maybe they are right."

Keiko rose from her chair after leaving enough money on the table to pay for her food and drinks.

"Want some advice, Harlan? Plenty of other hobbies out there. Why don't you find something else? Just don't get into knitting or crocheting. If you were my boyfriend, I'd have a hard enough time explaining to people you like searching for aliens in your spare time. Crocheting? Not going to happen. See you next week."

Harlan remained staring at his beer as Keiko got up and left. He sipped at it slowly, dwelling on his frustration. Five minutes later Carrie finally came over and stood by the table to catch his attention. After a long moment she finally spoke.

"Harlan? Did you want another?"

Harlan finally came out of his reverie. "No, I don't think so. Going to head home."

"Struck out with her, huh?"

Harlan gave her a small, rueful smile in reply as he looked up at her. Everyone knew Carrie well, because she was a fixture at The Lamp, having been one of the servers there since the first day Harlan became a customer. He was certain she was well into her fifties in age and, without doubt, had seen it all at The Lamp.

"Well, I wouldn't call it striking out, but I haven't hit a home run yet either. Far from it."

"You're a good-looking guy and there's lots of fish out there, Harlan. Don't give up hope. Say, changing the topic here, and just out of curiosity, did you see that guy staring at your table earlier?"

"A guy staring at our table? No. When was this?"

"Right after you came in. I wouldn't have paid him any mind, except he stopped in the entrance and just stood there looking over at your table for a little while. Well, that and the fact he never took his hat or sunglasses off. The sun was almost down when you came in, so I don't know why he felt the need for either. And then he just turned and left after a minute or so, without doing or saying anything."

"Weird. I don't know what that was about, but if he shows up again, let us know, I guess. Anyway, I'm going to hit the road."

After paying his bill, Harlan left to make his home. And once again, the van pulled out to slowly follow him surreptitiously down the street.

***

On reaching his apartment Harlan wearily changed out of his work clothes into more comfortable shorts and a t-shirt. He stared at the fridge for a moment trying to decide if he should have one more beer and the decision wasn't long in coming. The night was pleasant and he needed to wind down from his week. Somehow going back up to the roof to stare at the anomaly once more gave him no joy, given the frustration he was still feeling.

Making his way out to his patio deck with a new glass of beer, he slumped into a chair to watch the people and the cars go by on the street. He wasn't sitting there long when the familiar bulk of Spock landed in his lap. The cat began walking about, looking to find the most comfortable way to sit down, before he finally settled and began purring loudly.

"God, Spock, don't do that. Damn near spilled my beer."

"Spock? Where...oh, there you are, you little monster. Leave Harlan alone," said a nearby voice.

Harlan turned and saw Isaac standing on the other side of the small barrier that separated their tiny patios.

"He's okay, Isaac. He just surprised me again. How are you doing? If you're having a nightcap why don't you come over and join me?"

"A fine idea. Let me grab my drink."

Moments later Isaac walked around the barrier, putting his own glass full of beer on the table beside Harlan's. Spock jumped down and looked up at Isaac, who picked up the cat and put him in his lap.

"Silly puss. I think you spend more time over here with Harlan than you do with me."

But the cat was no longer purring or paying

attention to either of them. Spock was standing up again and was staring hard out at the street, his tail whisking back and forth. To Harlan's surprise the cat even began growling deep in his throat. Harlan tried to figure out what was putting the cat on edge, but he saw no obvious reason for it. All he could see was a few people walking down the street and a nondescript looking dark van which was moving slowly past their location in an apparent effort to find a parking spot. Oddly, the cat's attention seemed focused on following the van.

"Wow, what's up with Spock, Isaac?"

Even as he finished speaking Harlan realized both Isaac and the cat were staring hard at the van, which was now further down the street. After what seemed close to a minute Isaac finally replied as it turned and disappeared around the street corner, although both he and Spock were now looking at each other and not Harlan as he spoke.

"Hmm, nothing, nothing. It was just nothing, right, Spock?" said Isaac as he put the cat down. The two of them stared at each other for another brief moment, making Harlan raise a questioning eyebrow, before both of them turned away. Isaac moved over to sit down in the chair beside Harlan.

"Who knows with cats? Maybe he heard a dog or a raccoon or something. So, I haven't seen you out here for a while. I've been getting used to having our nightcaps on the patio together. Where have you been? You look tired."

Harlan sighed as several possible responses ran through his mind. A part of him wanted to spill all of his frustrations out and tell him everything, but another part of him felt discouraged and tired.

"I am tired, Isaac. Long week at work and I was up late looking at the stars again a few nights this week. I'm heading out of town early tomorrow morning to see my folks and I'll be back Sunday. So it'll be an early night for me."

"Sure. Find anything interesting out there?" said Isaac, pointing up at the sky.

"Well, actually, yes. Sort of. But I don't know what to make of it. I think I told you a while back I follow the SETI stuff, didn't I? Never told you much about it. I guess I should have, huh? You are obviously a sci-fi fan if you have a cat named Spock. Well, it's a long story. I'll fill you in next week."

"You sound frustrated."

Harlan sighed. "I am. I was debating whether to tell my friends about it and, courtesy of Spock here, the email got sent before I made up my mind."

"Spock? Good Lord, what did he do?"

As Harlan explained what happened Isaac stared down at Spock, who responded by once again jumping into Isaac's lap. Once the cat settled down and began purring, Harlan could have sworn Spock was wearing the same strange grin on his face as two nights before when the email was sent. Like they did minutes before, Isaac and the cat shared a long look at each other.

"Right, so let me guess," said Isaac, raising an eyebrow at the cat as he spoke. "Whatever it was, they didn't believe you, did they?"

"You got that right. It's why I was thinking long and hard about whether to send it. Anyway, it's done. I just wish I'd gotten a little more support than I did."

Isaac stared at him in silence for a moment before taking a casual sip at his beer.

"Okay, I'm going to take another shot in the dark, here. Was one of them a particular lady you were hoping to impress?"

Harlan sighed and turned to eye Isaac, before taking his own deep pull at his beer.

"Don't know how you figured that out, but you got it the first time. Is it all that grey hair and experience you have?"

Isaac laughed. "Yes, indeed. Three ex-wives and almost sixty years under my belt. I've earned my grey hair, thank you."

"Three wives? Wow, the truth is I was wondering about your background. You mentioned the last time we were talking that you've lived all over the world. I confess I was secretly thinking you used to be a spy or maybe you're in a witness protection program or something. But perhaps the reason you moved here is more mundane. Dare I ask, you aren't dodging alimony are you?"

Isaac laughed again, harder this time.

"No, my ex-wives are all well taken care of and, no, I didn't have them murdered for the insurance money either. I started out working toward a career in academia, but joined the diplomatic corps instead, which is why I've lived in many different places. When I retired I decided to just keep going different places. I like to stay in a place for a little while and really get to know it before I move on. One of these days when I'm older I'll settle in one place."

"So what did you do as a diplomat?"

"Ah, if I told you that I'd have to kill you because it's all secret, of course. Nothing nefarious, just secret. Think of me as an assistant to ambassadors. Sometimes I'd operate on my own, in what you might call a branch office. Go into places where we may or may not want to open an office. I suppose I should clarify I still do the occasional contract jobs for my former employers."

"Right, so you're a spook of some sort. Hey, I can live with that, it's how the world works. Okay, no more questions about it. But the women wanted to stay in one place and build a nest, I expect?"

"Well, they were all very different in their own ways, but yes, I suppose that's as good a reason as any. I've just never felt a desire to settle in one place for long. Lots to see and do out there. But what's special about this lady that isn't interested in you?"

"Good question. She's smart and attractive. She has high standards. She's more than a bit jaded about men and life in general. She has a real sharp sense of humour and doesn't suffer fools gladly. I can't pin down exactly why, but I've been attracted to her for years. I think the adjective wild would best describe her when she was younger and, of course, she wanted nothing to do with a nerd like me. She has always been way more outgoing, where I am the opposite. Deep down, we really are very similar people, though. This may sound weird, but it feels like I've been patiently waiting for her to one day wake up and see that I'm the man for her."

"Still hasn't happened, huh. Well, there's lots of

other women out there. Look at me, I managed to catch three of them. But doesn't it feel like it's finally time to move on if she isn't really interested?"

Harlan shrugged. "You're the second person to suggest that to me today. Well, I've had other relationships, but they never worked out. And all the while I just kept wanting her. God, I know, that probably makes me some kind of head case. Any advice?"

"No, you're just a human, and no, I have no advice. Listen, I'm the guy that has three ex-wives, remember? But if it floats your boat to keep the flame alive for her then I'd say go for it."

Harlan stared at the remnants of his beer for a long moment before downing what was left.

"Fair enough, Isaac. Listen, I really am bagged and I am getting up early tomorrow. Love to chat with you another night."

"Yes, time to go," said Isaac, taking the cue to down his own drink. Picking Spock up from his lap as he rose from his chair he made to leave. He stopped at the barrier between their patios and turned back for a moment, pointing to the sky as he spoke.

"And before I forget, I would very much like to hear more about what you found out there. As you suspected, you are right that Spock and I are both big science fiction fans. Aren't we, Spock?"

Harlan watched as Isaac and the cat looked at each other.

"Meooww!" said Spock right on cue, as if the cat understood exactly what Isaac was talking about.

"Well, I'm glad at least someone wants to know more about what I've uncovered," said Harlan, as he waved goodbye and went inside, thinking the two of them were a rather strange pair. But it was comforting to know at least someone was interested in his discovery.

Chapter Four

Harlan's weekend trips to the nearby town a few hours away where his parents now lived were always a blur and whenever he went to visit he was left feeling as if nothing was left of his weekend at all. The Monday starting his week back at work carried on from where it left off on the Friday before, leaving him feeling just as tired at the end of the day and he still hadn't done everything he needed to do.

To save himself some time and because he was too tired to face cooking for himself anyway, Harlan decided to take a laptop from work and headed to The Lamp for a quick dinner. Instead of spending time in his own kitchen he knew he could use the opportunity to finish his work while they prepared his meal.

He waved at Carrie as he came in the door and this time made for one of the small, empty, two person booths, while outside the strange van still following him about drove slowly past. As much as he wanted a beer, he declined when Carrie asked him and ordered a glass of water instead along with a clubhouse sandwich.

As Carrie bustled off to place the order Harlan powered up the laptop and set to work. Carrie reappeared and dropped off the water glass as the van outside finally found a parking stall, having been forced to drive around the block in search of one. This time it was much further from the entrance, but the spot still afforded a distant view of inside The Lamp through the big exterior glass windows.

Harlan was deeply engrossed in his work on the laptop five minutes later when someone slipped into the seat across from him at the table. He looked up and was surprised to see an old man sitting there looking back at him showing obvious interest clearly on his face. The old man was completely unfamiliar to him. Harlan needed a moment to process what was happening, for although he could tell something was odd about the old man, he couldn't quite place what it was.

Harlan's attention was at first drawn to the grey-haired old man's face, which was gnarled and lined to significant degree. The strange part was although he was certain his initial impression this man earned his appearance through many hours spent outside, his skin at the moment wasn't any more tanned than Harlan's was. The immediate conclusion that the old man therefore wasn't spending time outside recently was supported by a quick look at his bare arms, for they too were not particularly tanned.

As he focused on the appearance of the old man's hands and arms, Harlan realized it reinforced the impression this man at some point in his life worked outdoors doing manual labour. The man's hands were even more lined and weathered than his face, while his bare arms were heavily corded with muscle. Despite being obviously old enough to be Harlan's grandfather, he was certain this old man was also strong enough to pick him up and throw him across the room if he wanted to.

Harlan was about to speak and ask the old man what he wanted when it finally hit him why something seemed odd about his appearance. The old man was wearing a checked short-sleeve shirt of a style no one ever wore now. Harlan recalled seeing pictures of people back in the mid twentieth century wearing the style, but that was long ago.

And while it was odd enough to be wearing a shirt that was a common enough sight among blue collar working people from decades past, what was really strange was the shirt was inside out.

"Hello, son," said the old man. "Hope you don't mind if I join you for a bit?"

"Uhh...," said Harlan, rapidly trying to decide just how crazy the old man was. "Well, okay, I suppose. Can I help you with something?"

"Yes, I certainly hope so. I..."

The old man got no farther as Carrie dropped Harlan's sandwich on the table in front of him. She turned to look at the old man, wearing what Harlan was certain could only be the same puzzled look about the old man's shirt as Harlan knew was on his own face a few moments ago. But having seen it all in her years at The Lamp, the only definitive sign of her curiosity was a raised eyebrow.

"Good evening, sir. Can I get you anything?"

"Just a glass of water, please."

"Water. Okay, do you need a menu?"

"No, just water, thank you."

Carrie shrugged and nodded before turning away. As she did she shared a quick, puzzled glance with Harlan. As Harlan turned back the old man pointed at the plate of food in front of him.

"Please, don't let me stop you from enjoying your meal. I can talk while you listen, if that's okay."

Harlan stared at the old man for a long moment, before eyeing the sandwich in front of him as his stomach growled. He pushed his laptop to the side and reached for the sandwich as he spoke.

"Okay, you talk, I will eat. You said I can help you somehow?"

"Possibly. Say, I like this place. It reminds me of some of the old diners we used to have back home. Don't see many places like this anymore, do you?"

With his mouth full of sandwich Harlan could only nod his head in agreement as the old man continued talking.

"So I guess I should introduce myself before I go any further. My name is Arthur. I used to be a farmer, although I suppose I still am in a way. Being a farmer is a way of life and, who knows, maybe I can get back to doing what I love one day. You don't need to introduce yourself, I already know your name is Harlan. What I would like is to know a lot more about you and that's why I'm here today."

Arthur stopped talking as Harlan raised an eyebrow in question. Since he was halfway through his sandwich, he used the time to finish chewing his last big bite and process what the old man said before speaking.

"So, Arthur, how is it exactly you already know my name? And for that matter, why do you want to know more about me?"

"It was your email, of course. You found me. And as to why, well, that's a bit of a long story, but I assure you it will make sense once you hear it."

"My email? What email? I don't know what you are talking about."

"Of course you do. You found my flying saucer. You mentioned the coordinates in your email to your friends, which is why I know your name and could find you."

Harlan shook his head and rubbed his face in disbelief, which must have been obvious from the look on his face, because it prompted the old man to give him the coordinates to prove what he was saying. Knowing they were correct, Harlan's jaw fell open as he sat back in the booth still in shock. He sat there long enough for a concerned look to appear on the old man's face.

"You okay, son?"

Harlan shook his head again. "Okay? About as okay as I could be while thinking I'm in some kind of bizarre waking dream or maybe even an alternative universe. Look, seriously, how do you know those coordinates? Did someone put you up to this? One of my friends, I expect."

"Someone put me up to this? Heavens, no. I told you, I got them from your email."

"Sure. Okay. And exactly how is it you can intercept and read my emails?"

The old man shrugged. "Probably the same way the government does it. They aren't the only ones that can do that. Well, the ship does the work for me. Must be this new-fangled...what do they call it these days? Yeah, this artificial intelligence I keep hearing about. Anyway, the ship monitors all this stuff and tells me when I have to pay attention."

"So your flying saucer's computers do this? And

you get a message. Really."

"Well, I suppose they are computers. Alien versions, of course. I'm not much of an expert on them. I know way more about tractors and farm implements. I could tell you plenty about those if you want."

"Okay, sure. If nothing else, it makes sense a farmer would know about farm stuff. But I have to tell you, old man, or I think you said your name is Arthur, nothing else you are saying makes any bloody sense. You're going to have to do way better than this to explain what is going on, because I am still thinking this is the most bizarre dream I've had in a long time. And hopefully I will wake up shortly."

"I'll try. But your sandwich and fries are getting cold. Please do eat them."

Harlan shook his head in disbelief once again, but his stomach was still telling him he was hungry so he reached for another quartered piece of his sandwich and began eating again. Between bites he asked another question.

"So why don't you tell me about this flying saucer of yours, Arthur? I'm listening."

"Hmm. Kind of hard to describe. My wife Ursula and I live there. Seems to be plenty of room for us, although I don't think it's actually all that big a ship. Lots of gadgets and stuff I have no idea what they do. But we've had a good life on the ship. Everything we could want is there for us. The ship is real fast. Never seems to be a lack of stuff for us to do. My wife even has a room she can do her gardening in, so she's happy."

"God Almighty," said Harlan, having wolfed down the last of his sandwich and most of his fries. He pushed the plate to the side and stared at the old man.

"Okay, here's a real question for you. Why are you wearing your shirt inside out?"

The old man looked down and fingered his shirt for a few moments, before turning back to Harlan with an embarrassed look on his face.

"Well, darn, you're right. Guess I was in a hurry to meet you. Of course, I don't wear clothes much anymore, so I'm out of practice. No need to wear much in the saucer, you see. The temperature is controlled perfectly so we are never too hot or cold. Next time I'll get my wife to check me out first."

"Huh. Well, I suppose in a bizarre way that makes sense. If I assume you really are living on a flying saucer, of course. So here's another question for you. Who is it the military pilots keep seeing sometimes and occasionally take pictures of? Is that you? And if so, how come they don't see you more often?"

"Oh, that's easy. Most of the time the ship is in what it calls hide mode. All that anyone can see is maybe perhaps a little wobble in their field of sight, like what happened to you as you said in your email. A lot of the alleged pictures of alien spaceships out there are just junk. I think a bunch of them are just old-style car hubcaps that people with a sense of mischief in them used to fake as being flying saucers. But the ship lets me play with it sometimes when I get bored. I like to toy with the fly boys in the military once in a while and show them who's the boss. Give them a day they won't soon forget, you know, just a little fun. So if it's a military picture, it's far more likely to be the real thing."

"The ship lets you play with it, you say."

"Sure. Listen, if you owned a real fast hot rod, wouldn't you want to take it out for a spin once in a while? Of course you would. So I turn the hide function off and take her out. She can fly circles around them. But I can't do it that often. The ship tells me when I can. We aren't trying to draw attention to ourselves, of course. On the other hand, I do get to take it other places sometimes, too."

"Other places?"

"Yeah, most of the time the ship wants to be in the...what do you call it... geostationary orbit you found us in, but it lets us take it on little side trips. Think of it as going for dinner out with the wife, but instead of walking down the street we take the ship there."

Arthur paused a moment before continuing, a fond look of remembrance appearing on his face.

"We've both developed a taste for Greek food! Don't get anything like that in the little farm town near where we used to live. The most exotic restaurant they have is a Chinese food place with kind of a basic menu, although the food is usually decent enough. Gets a little boring eating it all the time, though. On the other hand, a great prawn or chicken souvlaki dinner sitting in a restaurant on the rim of the caldera in Santorini can't be beat. Ever been there? We highly recommend it. I can give you the names of a few restaurants to try. We've been to several other countries for dinner out on lots of other nights, too."

"No, I've not been there. If I ever get my own flying saucer to take me there I'll get a hold of you and we can meet for dinner," replied Harlan, a sarcastic tone to his voice, before he continued without pause.

"Okay, look, before this whole conversation gets any loonier than it already is, I think you said you want to know more about me. I have no idea why, but I expect you have some kind of reason. Explain, please."

"Sure. You are correct, I do have reasons for this. But before I get into it, I have a few questions for you. I think this will all make sense when I'm done. So, how did you manage to find me and why?"

Harlan sighed, taking a few moments to explain about the SETI source material and how he found the anomaly in their data which he couldn't explain. When he finished, he shrugged his shoulders.

"As to why, well, it was a mystery. So I took the time to check it out."

"Okay, but why are you looking at this SETI information in the first place?"

Harlan stared at the old man for a long moment before responding with what he thought was obvious sarcasm in his voice.

"Good God, what do you think? I was looking for ET. Don't you think it would be logical to look for extra-terrestrials in SETI data?"

The old man smiled. "Bear with me. Why are you interested in finding extra-terrestrials? What is motivating your search?"

"What is...uh," said Harlan, pausing because the words simply wouldn't come. Still struggling for an answer moments later, a silence descended between the two of them. He let his head fall to stare at the table as he thought about it, feeling how tired he was as he did.

On the surface, the question seemed simple enough, but in reality much more was behind it. The first problem coming to mind was no one ever asked him why he spent so much time working his way through the SETI data and, as a result, he never needed to articulate it properly. Everyone simply accepted this was what he wanted to do.

The second problem he now faced was the reality no clear event in his life was driving him to do this. Over time he simply gravitated toward doing it as a hobby and he stuck with it. Searching inside for an answer, one finally came to him. Raising his head, he looked at the old man once again.

"I think...yes, I'd say I do this because I'm searching for meaning. Searching for purpose. Searching for order. This world is a pretty crazy place. Sometimes things happen logically and sometimes things happen that make no sense whatsoever. I think it all means there is more to this than meets the eye, so I wanted to look for answers. I figure some of those answers might be out there in the great beyond. Once we have answers, we can maybe sort things out down here. I don't know, that's probably as good an explanation as any and it's all you're going to get from me tonight."

"Ah, so you want to sort things out down here. In

other words, you care about what happens around you, right? You'd like to make things better?"

"Well, sure. Who doesn't?"

"Oh, you'd be surprised. Not everyone cares about anything other than themselves. But I'm a farmer. I like to grow things and take care of things. I like to be helpful and I think you do, too. Yes, I think you can help me."

"Help, you say. Right."

Harlan stared at the old man once again and as he did the whole bizarre conversation simply became too overwhelming to deal with, especially as tired as he was. Harlan reached into his pocket for his wallet and threw a wad of bills on the table to pay for his dinner. As a surprised look appeared on the face of the old man Harlan pulled his laptop over, put it into his backpack, and he slipped out of the booth.

"Where are you going? We have more to talk about."

"Well, maybe you do, but I am done for the day, Arthur. Look, I'm sorry, I'm really tired and I still have work to get done before the night is out, so I'm going home to finish it. And I'm still hoping this is all just some really weird, long dream I'm going to wake up from soon."

"Okay, I'd like to come and see you again. We still have much to discuss."

Harlan sighed and gave his head a shake. "Of course we do. Apparently this is some endless dream that will pick up where it left off tomorrow or something. Good God. Look, it has been...interesting talking to you."

Harlan turned and waved at Carrie to catch her attention. When he was sure he'd caught her eye, he pointed at the cash on the table. As she waved acknowledgement he turned to leave.

"I'll be in touch," said the old man.

"Sure. You do that."

Outside, Harlan stopped to take a few deep breaths, as if he could clear his head in the fresh air before making his way home. And unlike previous occasions, the mysterious van remained parked where it was. Unseen by Harlan, first one man stepped out of the van and then another. They stood watching Harlan disappear down the street before turning to look back at The Lamp. To a casual observer, it would be obvious the two men were having a disagreement. One man finally pointed decisively at the diner, while the other shrugged in clear frustration. But the two men began making their way toward The Lamp.

***

Carrie finished cleaning up a couple of tables before finally making her way over to Harlan's booth to collect the money left for her. As she went she glanced outside and saw from the corner of her eye two men standing beside a strange looking van at the far end of the street having what appeared to be a heated discussion. A vague memory stirred and she looked again, as despite the distance one of the men appeared oddly familiar. Unable to be certain, she gave a mental shrug after a moment and focused her attention to the old man still sitting in the booth.

In itself, nothing was unusual about his remaining behind, but the fact he was sitting there talking to himself was another matter. Given the location of The Lamp in a tougher area of town, more than a few people in need of medication or those who were off their medications wandered in and did the same thing. She couldn't begin to count how many times it happened in the years since she began working there.

With practiced, wary caution she worked her way around to slowly draw near the old man from within his line of sight to ensure he wasn't surprised by her approach. Despite her certainty he could see her, he carried on talking as if she weren't there. Carrie stood warily beside the table for several long moments before he finally seemed to realize what was happening.

"Yes, yes, I am certain. Unfortunately, he...oh, hello," said the old man, finally looking up at Carrie. "Can I help you?"

Carried reached down and picked up the money, scooping it into the pocket of the apron she wore.

"Well, actually, I'm the one wondering if I can help you. Your friend left. Would you like something more than the glass of water? A menu, perhaps?"

The old man stared down at the water glass as if seeing it for the first time, before looking back up at her.

"Um, no, thank you. The water was fine and I don't need anything else. I forgot I was still here. I'll fix that and be gone shortly."

Carrie looked down at the still untouched glass of water and decided it was definitely time to make a retreat.

"Sure. Right. You just holler or wave if you change your mind, sir."

Carrie backed away from the table slowly, shaking her head in disbelief. She made her way behind the diner counter, where the other server on duty that night was standing and waiting for her. Her colleague nodded in the direction of the old man, still sitting there talking to himself.

"What's with him? Do we need to call the cops?"

Carrie surreptitiously looked behind her to see if the old man was watching her. Although he was still talking to himself, he wasn't watching her and she was certain he wouldn't hear her. She turned back to her colleague, whom she knew was relatively new and less experienced in dealing with customers like this. Carrie shrugged.

"No, I don't think so. Not yet, anyway. He seems harmless enough. He told me he was going to leave soon, so let's see what happens. It's not too busy tonight and we don't need the table. Trust me, we are better off to humour the loonies and hope they go away if at all possible. Sad to say, this isn't the first time we've had someone in here talking to themselves, although this guy seems to be having a proper conversation with an invisible companion. I haven't seen that in a long time. Anyway, with any luck he actually will leave soon."

Her colleague nodded warily and both of them went back to work on other tasks. Carrie was busy cleaning a table soon afterwards when she heard someone behind her speak.

"Sorry to interrupt what you are doing. Could you help me, please? I'm hoping you can answer a few questions."

Carrie turned and saw two men standing behind her, one black and one white. Both appeared to be in their mid-thirties in age. They also both wore jeans and casual shirts with an expensive look to them. One was slightly taller than the other, but both men looked equally fit. Neither of them seemed otherwise remarkable in any way except for the mirror sunglasses and ball caps both wore. With a flash of recognition Carrie realized the white man was the one who entered The Lamp to look around and then leave again the week before when Harlan and his friends were here.

"Um, sure. What can I do for you?"

"We'd like to know where the old man went. The one that was sitting over them a little while ago."

Carrie gave a start and turned to look at the booth Harlan and the old man were sitting at minutes before. To her surprise, the old man was indeed gone, although the glass of water was still sitting untouched on the table.

"Well, that's weird," said Carrie, walking over to the table to pick up the glass and look around in puzzlement. "He was here a minute ago. Hang on a second."

Carrie walked across the room and approached her colleague, who was just finishing taking another table's order. Carrie asked if she saw the old man leave, but the other server was as surprised he was gone as was Carrie. She went back to the two men and shrugged.

"Sorry. Neither of us saw him leave. It could only have been a couple of minutes ago at most, so he must have snuck out the front door."

"That's not possible. We were watching and came in through the front door ourselves. I guarantee he didn't leave that way. Are there other exits?"

Carrie frowned. "Well, sure, there's a side door over there, but it's always locked and he would need a key. The only other way out is through the kitchen at the back."

One of the men went over to the side door and tested it, but the door was still locked.

"He would have to be a magician to have gone that way. This has a deadbolt, too. He could have left by unlatching it, but I can't see how he would have been able to relock it. Could you check with your kitchen workers to see if he went that way, please?"

"Uh, sure. Give me a minute," said Carrie. She disappeared into the back and reappeared a couple of minutes later.

"Sorry, gentlemen. He definitely didn't go that way. There is no way he could have got past our kitchen staff without them seeing him. He has to have left by the front door."

The two men turned to each other, puzzled looks on their faces, before turning back to Carrie.

"Okay, fine. Let's drop that for now. Could you tell me what you saw please?"

"What I saw?" said Carrie, frowning. "Say, are you two cops or something? Did this guy do something bad?"

"Hmm...yes, well, you could say we have an interest in this man. We would prefer not to get into it. Please just assume we have a need to know and it would be helpful if you could just answer our questions."

"Need to know, huh?" Carrie eyed both men dubiously, but decided to simply do as they asked. She told them what she saw and heard, which in the end didn't seem like much. Oddly, both men seemed fascinated by the fact he was sitting there apparently talking to someone else.

"So let me make sure I have this straight," said one of the men. "You say you've never seen this old man before until today, correct?"

"That's right. We've had other people in here talking to themselves, but not this guy. Of course, the fellow he was talking to who left is Harlan. He's been in here many times."

"Yes, we already know who he is," said the other man. "Hmm...and you say the old man wore his shirt on inside out?"

"Yeah."

The two men fell silent and stood staring at each other for a long moment, before Carrie decided grew a little fed up with the questioning.

"Look gentlemen or officers or whoever you are. Any more questions? I have work to do. So if you are staying for dinner or drinks please find a table and I'll bring you a menu."

"Uh...no, we are leaving. Thanks for your help."

Carrie watched the two men leave before going back to where her colleague was standing behind the counter, having watched the entire scene.

"What was that all about?"

"Darned if I know, they wouldn't tell me

anything. Those two smell like cops to me, but they wouldn't admit it. You know, sometimes this place is boring as all hell, and other days it gets crazy. Have to say today falls into the downright crazy and strange category. We'll just have to see what kind of weirdness tomorrow brings."

Chapter Five

Harlan was tired again as he left work early the next day for a medical appointment. The problem was his day wasn't over yet, for he brought a work laptop with him to finish a job he needed done for first thing the next day at home that night. Walking through a park near his apartment on the way to his doctor's office he was lost in thought when he a strange sensation something or someone was walking beside him came. He stopped in his tracks and without turning his head he spoke aloud.

"It's you again, isn't it? Is this really some bizarre alternate universe I'm in?"

"As far as I know there is only one universe, but then who am I? I'm just a simple farmer, so I wouldn't take my word for it."

Harlan turned and stared at the old man standing beside him. Unlike the day before, this time he was wearing an old, floppy brown brim hat. Another simple, old style checked shirt was partially covered by the work overalls he wore. A pair of work boots were also on his feet. Despite looking like he could have just come from spending his day out in the fields, everything he wore was spotlessly clean. Harlan shook his head.

"Well, if it isn't that, this has got to be some really, really weird dream. Whatever, I'm in it now. And here you are again. Hey, at least this time you have your shirt on properly. Are you trying to deliberately dress the part? You look like you're ready to go work on the back forty."

The old man laughed. "Yeah, I made sure I was

dressed right today. I had the wife supervise me, if you can believe it. She thought it was most amusing that she needed to. And these are the clothes I always used to wear. Real comfortable. Nothing fancy for me."

"I'm sure. Look, Arthur, why are you stalking me? Really. Please give me the straight goods here."

"I told you yesterday, I'm interested in you because I think you can help."

"Help? God Almighty, Arthur, or whatever you are, you're going to have to do better than that. Let's see, you claim you live on a flying saucer. So right there that probably means you're in fact really an alien. And if that's the case, why don't you just abduct me? You likely have the means to do whatever you want. Take me off to probe me and make me do your bidding or whatever. So why don't you just get on with it? I have a doctor's appointment to go to if not."

"Well, first of all, I'm just as human as you are. And as far as abducting and probing you goes, well, I don't know. The alien hasn't done that for a long time, not since it happened to us. If anything more recent has happened it would have to be some other aliens doing it. My wife and I have never done any abducting or probing of anybody. I wouldn't know the first thing about probing you. I've probed a lot of cows in my time, but never a human. I suppose it couldn't be that much different, so if you want I guess I could ask the ship about doing it with you."

"Oh, really. This is getting more and more interesting, so I guess I do need to hear more. Now let me get this straight. You say both you and your wife were abducted and taken to the flying saucer, right? How exactly did that happen?"

"Yes, we were taken by surprise. I remember I was out in the field on our farm near Vulcan when it happened. It's all kind of fuzzy, but I vaguely remember these strange lights surrounding me. Next thing I knew I was on the ship with my wife beside me. My wife remembers being in the kitchen preparing dinner when the same thing happened to her."

"Vulcan? Isn't that a planet..."

Arthur laughed. "I knew you were going to say that. Everyone makes that mistake. Yes, it actually was the name of a fictional planet on television back in the sixties, as I'm sure you know, but in reality the town near my farm on the Prairies is named Vulcan and it has been around a lot longer. Look it up. We grow a lot of wheat and other crops in the area like canola, beans, corn, you name it. The town eventually built a mock spaceship to draw attention to themselves because of the name when the tv series came out. If a few people in Vulcan can make a buck off a few tourists, well, why not?"

"I'll take your word for it. Okay, let's see if I got this. The aliens really were abducting and probing people and, let me guess, this was back in the nineteen-fifties when there were all kinds of reports about it, right?"

"Exactly. That's when we were taken."

"Okay, so here's a question for you. Why were they abducting all these people? What about all the others?"

"Good question. I'm not real sure why, but the alien never kept all the other people. I figure they didn't meet the needs like my wife and I did."

"So you and your wife are it? Just you two in the one flying saucer?"

"Right. Far as I know, there aren't other aliens or humans around, but then maybe they are hiding like us."

"Naturally. These aliens seem to be good at hiding. And why exactly do you think the alien kept you two?"

"Well, it's never been real clearly explained, but I think it was because we both care. Like I told you yesterday, we like to be positive. We're farmers. We grow things and help people. We don't want to blow stuff up or have a war or anything like that. And I think you feel the same way."

"You're right about that," said Harlan, pausing for a moment to think. Something was nagging at him and as he stared at the old man it finally came to him.

"Listen, Arthur. Another question for you. So, how old were you when you were taken?"

"Oh, my wife and I were both in our early sixties."

"Early sixties?" said Harlan, his mouth falling open. "God Almighty, how does that work? If you were taken in the last century in the nineteen-fifties when you were sixty years old, you'd be somewhere around a hundred and twenty years old or more right now. Have to say, I can only wish I'm looking as good as you if I ever get to that age."

"Well, I told you, the alien probed us, right? Not

quite sure what all was done to us, but we really haven't aged a whole lot since that happened."

The old man paused and laughed. "My wife Ursula keeps telling me she wishes we'd been abducted when we were a bit younger. She doesn't like looking at the lines on her face in the mirror. She's asked the ship several times to do something about that with no luck so far. I tell her I still see the beauty queen I married regardless, so I'm happy."

"Uh huh. Of course," said Harlan, rubbing his face. "Look, here's another question for you. If you've been on the flying saucer that long, why hasn't the alien come back? Or did he come back and leave again?"

The old man shrugged. "I don't know. Honestly. Far as we know, the alien hasn't come back. If he did, I'm sure we would have known about it, but then maybe not. Who knows?"

"Right. Okay. So, you want me to help. What exactly are we talking about?"

"Yes, I need your help. See, my wife and I were given a job to do, which we have for many years. The thing is I'm getting a message from the ship it may finally be time to replace us and that I needed to start looking for someone to do that. The timing was great because I was just wondering how to go about that when I also got the message you found us. It seemed like a bit of...what do they call that again? Yeah, that serendipity thing. The universe works in funny ways, doesn't it?"

"God, you got that right. Look, Arthur, this is all fascinating, but I've got a doctor appointment to go to and I'm going to be late. Can we continue this later?"

"Sure, I'll find you tomorrow. But I actually do think you'd be great for this."

"I...wait, let me get this straight. You really are telling me you want me to replace you on the saucer?"

"Yes. That's exactly what I'm talking about. Like I said, I think you care about people and the future just like me. But there is one thing. It would get real lonely up there if it was just you. Are you by any chance thinking of getting married? Got anyone in mind?"

Harlan began laughing in response, unable to think of a possible response that made any sense. After a minute he finally got himself under control enough to reply.

"This is ridiculous. Part of me is standing here wondering why your omnipotent ship doesn't already know this. The other part of me doesn't know what to say or do, beyond heading off to my doctor appointment which I must get to. But look here, Arthur. I'm going to need some kind of proof of all this and then I'm going to have to think about it all, long and hard. And now I'm off. If we really must continue this bizarre, alternate universe conversation then come and find me tomorrow. Goodbye."

Harlan turned and began walking away as the old man called after him.

"No problem. Take your time thinking about it. I will come and find you tomorrow."

"God help me, I'm sure you will," said Harlan, without looking back.

As he made his way further down the street with his mind abuzz, Harlan slowly became aware of a vehicle coming his way towards him that slowed to a crawl as it got closer. Despite the confusion fogging his brain it was impossible for him not to register its presence. He finally turned his full attention to it and frowned as he did, for the strange array of small antennas on the roof of the dark van made it stand out. The windows were lightly tinted just enough he couldn't possibly make out the exact features of the two people inside. On the other hand, he could tell by the outline of their bodies that both of them were staring directly at him.

Harlan walked a short ways further down the street trying to decide whether to simply keep ignoring it or to confront whoever was inside. By the time he drew almost level with the vehicle Harlan made up his mind he'd had enough of whatever was happening. He came to a full stop on the sidewalk and turned to face the van, standing with arms folded to wait and see what developed. The van continued driving by slowly, so Harlan pulled out his phone and took a picture of it. As he did the occupants in the van realized what he was doing and they sped up, driving off past him in the opposite direction Harlan was going in. Harlan raised both hands wide and shouted after the van as it passed him.

"What? Looking for me?"

With no response, Harlan shook his head and turned away. After checking the time on his phone and realizing he was now perilously close to being late, he began making his way back down the street.

He was only a short distance when he found he couldn't resist turning to see if the van really was gone.

To his surprise, the van was now parked much further down the street, across from the spot Harlan last saw the old man. Two men wearing ball caps and sunglasses came out and, to Harlan's utter disbelief, they began a hurried search of the area. Despite knowing he was late, he watched as they quickly scoured the area, searching behind bushes and trees, before finally turning to make their way back to the van. The old man was nowhere to be seen. Harlan shook his head to himself.

"Huh. If this is a dream, it's the most lucid one I've ever had. And God help me, I have a strange feeling this weirdness just might carry on again tomorrow."

He decided to wave goodbye to the two men before he turned away. Neither of them acknowledged it, but Harlan was certain they saw him, for both men were looking his direction as they got back in the vehicle. Once they were inside the van started up and drove away into the distance.
***

Later that evening Harlan finally closed his laptop with a groan and sat back in his desk chair. After rubbing his tired eyes he looked at the time and debated whether to allow himself a beer before crawling off to bed. As it was a nice evening he decided he would, so he poured himself a drink and went outside.

He was unsurprised to find his neighbour already out on the edge of his own patio, holding Spock in his arms and staring out down the street. Harlan watched as Isaac muttered something to Spock before putting him down and turning to wave at Harlan. Isaac waved him over as he went to sit down at the table, while Spock disappeared off into the bushes.

"Evening, Harlan. I was wondering if you were coming out tonight. Why don't you come on over and enjoy my patio?"

Without speaking Harlan made his way across to Isaac's patio and slumped into the deck chair across from his neighbour, taking a long pull at his beer after sitting down.

"You look tired again, if I may say," said Isaac.

"I am. Too much work, too many late nights. Too much weird shit going on in my life."

"Weird shit? Well, that sounds interesting. You said the other night you found something odd. Tell me how weird it really is."

Unburdening himself to Isaac about the events of the last week felt cathartic. Isaac remained mostly silent the whole time, interrupting him only briefly a couple of times to ask small questions. By the time Harlan finished telling him the whole story he realized to his dismay his entire glass of beer was gone. As he stared in surprise at the bottom of his empty glass, Isaac laughed.

"Apparently it was thirsty work, telling me all that. Here, why don't you have another on me. Give me a second and I'll get you one. I'll sort out which of the questions I've got for you to start with."

"I...sure, why not. I was only going to have the one, but maybe I deserve a second one tonight."

When Isaac returned with a full bottle in hand he waited until Harlan finished pouring his drink before speaking.

"So, that's a hell of a story and I agree with you, even if it is just a strange dream which may not be over yet. Seriously, how do you feel about it all?"

"Feel? Good question. I keep telling myself this is just totally weird, but it honestly feels to me like it's not a dream. But how that's possible, I have no idea. You know what the irony is here?"

"Tell me."

"The irony is I've been searching and hoping for a long time that I'd be the one to find an alien or aliens out there, but now that I may really have found an alien, I'm having a hard time believing it. Go figure."

"The problem is this old man says he isn't an alien, of course."

"Right. And he doesn't seem like one to me, but there's enough crazy pieces to this I could be wrong. He does admit to having been probed, whatever that means. Maybe this probing altered him enough he qualifies as an honest to God, bonafide alien. Damn, I don't know. You see my dilemma."

"I do. And, of course, none of this is happening anything like you imagined it might, correct?"

"Exactly. I was expecting...well, actually, I'm not sure now what the hell I was expecting now I think about it. But it wasn't this. So look, Isaac, you seem like a reasonably sane person. What do you think?"

Isaac smiled. "Oh, I believe there are aliens out there. They could be out there watching us even now as I speak. I like to keep an open mind about stuff."

"But in my case?"

"Sure, this is all possible. Why not? I don't think you are a lunatic, if that is what you are asking, and this is certainly interesting. Look, the last time I checked, they estimate the Milky Way has somewhere around well over a hundred billion stars in it, with plenty of planets attached to them. And that's just the galaxy this planet is in. There are countless other galaxies further out in space, which all presumably have stars with planets. So it really is ridiculous to assume this one little planet would be the only one to harbour life of some sort. But you know all this, of course. And despite the fact it all seems to be unfolding a little different than you thought it might, I suggest just go with the flow, so to speak."

"Yes, you're right. I do know all that, but the other side of that is if the possibilities are endless regarding other life out there, how come we haven't encountered them before now? Wasn't there some scientist that asked the question 'where is everybody' decades ago?"

"Indeed there was and it's a good question. Who knows, maybe you will be the one to answer that. If this fellow Arthur really is an alien, I expect sooner or later he will explain why he's been sitting in orbit for decades. If nothing else, I recommend asking him what exactly his task has been all these years."

"Good point, he never did actually explain that, although I suppose part of that is my fault since I haven't stuck around long when he has showed up."

"On the other hand, the obvious reason no one

has found aliens is likely because they don't want you find them. Why they don't want you to find them is another matter. Could be lots of reasons why not."

"Not the least of which may be that humans as a race aren't ready for it. God knows if I was an alien, I'd think long and hard about it. And then, of course, there's these bastards that seem to be following me around. What do you make of them?"

Isaac rubbed his face and stood up to stretch just as a car horn began honking loudly further down the street. Walking over to the edge of his patio he stared down the street to where the mystery van was parked, out of Harlan's sight from where he was sitting because of a tree in the way. What Harlan also couldn't see was Spock standing on the front hood of the van peeing on the window, as the two men inside gave up on honking their horn and were now both struggling to get out to shoo him away. Isaac smiled as he turned back to face Harlan.

"Anything of interest happening out there?" said Harlan.

"No, looks like some dispute over who gets a parking stall. Ah, I felt the need to get up and stretch again. Can't let these old bones sit too long in one place. Anyway, as for this strange van, who knows? I suppose they could be aliens too, but I don't know why they would need a weird looking van or why they would be following you. Of course, they could be working for the government in some capacity. That's what I would put my money on."

"Yeah, that thought crossed my mind too, but why would they suddenly be following me right when this old guy claiming to live on a flying saucer shows up?"

"Well, if the old guy can read your emails, perhaps they did too."

"I hadn't considered that possibility. Shit, am I in trouble here?"

"Hmm, I wouldn't think so, but one never knows. Fortunately, this isn't a totalitarian state. If they were going to haul you away for questioning they would have done that already. So if they keep after you I suggest just continue to do what you've already been doing. Draw attention to them. If they really are doing something covert, attention is the last thing they want. And if they aren't going to arrest you or something, then politely tell them to get lost."

"Yeah, that sounds like good advice."

"On the other hand, if they happen to actually be aliens themselves, they might take offense at being told to get lost. Hmm. Well, I'll put my money on them being the cops of some description."

Spock reappeared from around the tree and came over to Isaac, who picked him up. Although his view was partially obscured, Harlan got the strange sense the two of them were both grinning at each other. Isaac made his way back to his chair with the cat in his arms and sat down once again. Spock promptly settled into his lap and began purring loudly while Isaac scratched behind his ears. He gave Harlan a questioning look as he did.

"So I'm curious about matters with your friends? You didn't say anything about that, but it sure seemed important to you the other night. Have you seen any of them since all this happened?"

"No, actually. And to be honest, I haven't figured out how to explain all this to them yet. You at least have an open mind, but those guys? Tough audience."

"The lady you want to impress the toughest of all, naturally. But let me see if I got this straight? The old man suggested you should be married, I think you said?"

"Yeah. If I can assume for a moment this isn't all some kind of opium dream, it actually makes sense he would suggest that. If he really is looking to replace himself and I end up on this flying saucer...God, I can't believe I'm saying this...if I end up there for as long as he's been there, I expect it would get rather lonely, wouldn't it?"

"Right. So how does the thought of moving into this flying saucer specifically with your lady friend for several decades sound? Does it feel right?"

Harlan was about to speak and then stopped himself, taking another pull of his now almost empty second glass of beer to buy himself time to think. After a few more long moments, he looked at Isaac.

"Yes. Yes, I think it does."

"Well, there you have it. That would be a good sign. Now you just have to convince her of the idea too."

"Easier said than done."

"Ah, but I think you do have a way to deal with both problems you have. First, you want to convince your friends this all isn't a large, smelly pile of horse crap, right? Second, and in particular, you want your lady friend to see you weren't just off chasing after some pipe dreams and to truly see you as a serious option."

"Sure. Go on."

"Well, wouldn't the solution be to just get your alien to prove it?"

"Prove it? Well, sure. How would he do that, do you think?"

Isaac shrugged. "Darned if I know. But that isn't your problem, is it? He's the one claiming to be something that on the surface seems preposterous. And whatever he does to prove it to you, he'll need to do it for your friends, won't he? Your lady friend in particular."

"Hmm, I like the way you think," said Harlan, finishing the last of his drink and rising from his chair. "I'll give it a shot."

"Did this fellow Arthur say when he would see you again?" said Isaac, rising from his chair too.

"He said he'd find me tomorrow."

"May I suggest something else? Find a way to be alone somewhere. I suspect he is happy enough to talk to you on your own. And I'd make a point of ensuring your mystery van is nowhere in sight."

"All good advice and suggestions. I'll take them. Well, I'm off to bed. I'll keep you posted."

And what Harlan didn't see as he walked away out of sight was Isaac making his way with Spock over to the edge of the patio to look down the street once more. The mystery van was still parked there, but the two occupants were now taking turns pouring buckets of water on the windshield of the van to try and dissipate the smell of cat pee.

Both Isaac and Spock smiled.

Chapter Six

The next day was sunny and warm, which worked well with Harlan's decision to bring a lunch and go to a nearby park on his break from work. Harlan enjoyed going to this park because there were usually very few people about and it held plenty of space to spread out with no one else nearby.

The mystery van made an appearance almost as soon as he sat down at one of the many large picnic tables clustered together in a big central clearing. Harlan scowled in the van's direction as it kept moving slowly down the street and he kept the scowl on his face until it was finally out of sight. Harlan remained staring after it, but to his surprise it didn't reappear.

Satisfied it wasn't coming back, Harlan opened his lunch kit and began to eat. What he didn't see was the van was now parked out of sight and the two occupants were making their way to a clump of brush close enough to Harlan they could watch him and still remain undetected.

The decision to take Isaac's advice and make himself available in a secluded location paid off as Arthur appeared once again, quietly slipping into the seat across from him at the picnic table. The old man smiled and said hello as Harlan looked around to ensure they weren't being observed before returning the greeting.

"So I'm hoping you have a little time for me today? Have you given thought to what I told you yesterday?"

"I have indeed and, yes, I have some questions," said Harlan, in between small bites of his sandwich. "I get the concept you somehow want me to replace you, but why that would be is still rather foggy. It also begs the question of what will happen to you if I was to do that. But look, I think the real question is what exactly it is that you do? What is your task, Arthur?"

"All good questions. The task is quite simple and most of your questions are easy enough to answer, but not all. I'm here to watch. Well, there is a little more to it than that. I have to make real sure we don't blow ourselves up."

"What do you mean, 'don't blow ourselves up'?" said Harlan, his mouth hanging open in surprise.

"You know. Humans destroying the world. Nuclear weapons, that stuff."

"Good God, are you serious?"

The old man looked puzzled, but nodded his head. "Of course."

Harlan put the remains of his sandwich down and put a hand to his forehead in frustration.

"Why is it every time I talk to you the conversation gets more and more bizarre? No, don't answer that. Okay, look, I've swallowed the hook already. You might as well tell me exactly why the alien or aliens don't want us to blow up. For that matter, why are you the one in charge of making sure we don't blow up?"

Arthur looked apologetic. "Sorry, I can't help you with those particular answers. I know that must sound odd, but I really have no idea. All I know is if it appears we are about to blow ourselves into oblivion, I have to stop it. Naturally, the ship will help, of course."

"Arthur, this is making no sense whatsoever. If the aliens are so all powerful they have a fancy flying saucer which can hide from everyone, let alone kidnap people and do something that keeps them alive way past a normal human lifespan, then what the hell do they need someone like you for to stop us from exterminating ourselves? No offense, you understand."

"None taken. Gee, I'd like to help you with that, but I have no answer. You'd have to ask the alien."

Harlan groaned. Reaching for his sandwich, he wolfed the rest of it down and began munching on an apple with one hand. He tapped the fingers of his other hand on the picnic table as he stared in thought at the old man who was sitting in silence with a patient look on his face. After finally finishing it and wiping his mouth, Harlan took a swig from his coffee mug and spoke again.

"Right. I have so many questions I'm not sure where to start, so I think to keep my sanity I'm going to stick to one question at a time. So you say I'd have to ask the alien, eh? When was the last time you saw the alien?"

"Back when we were abducted, like I told you. And to be clear, my memories of that are rather poor. If you're going to ask what he looked like, don't bother. All I remember is a very fuzzy, blurry kind of face."

"I see. So no contact since then."

"None."

"And if that's the case, how do you know it's

finally time to find a replacement?"

"I got a message from the ship, as I said."

"Okay, and how did you get it."

"Well, it appeared in my head. I expect that's because of whatever the alien put in me. Anyway, I've long since learned not to waste time wondering how it works, because the answer to that never comes. I confess I was kind of wondering how long this would go on, but it's become clear the ship wants me to find a replacement."

"I see. And what exactly is going to become of you if I end up replacing you."

"Gee, I don't know. The wife and I aren't losing a lot of sleep over it, though. We've enjoyed a good long life and I'm pretty sure the alien will find something for us to do. Or maybe we're just too old now and the alien's technology can't keep us alive anymore. Who knows? But we can't complain."

"Of course. So let's move on from that. I'm to replace you and this means I'm going to get probed and have implants or God knows what stuck in me too, is that right? Is this going to be painful or just plain weird like everything else to do with you?"

"Hmm. Good question. I don't remember it being painful or anything. It was all kind of blurry and dream like. My wife never said anything about it being painful either."

"But I am going to get probed or something?"

"I expect so. The ship hasn't sent a message about that, but I'll see if I can get an answer. Sometimes I ask questions and it takes time for the response to come. Sometimes I don't get answers. It's a mystery."

"It sure is. Look, I don't get this. If the ship is the boss and both you and it want me, why doesn't it just grab me like it did to you? Just get on with the probing stuff?"

The old man shrugged. "I don't know. There were a bunch of people abducted and probed before me and my wife. Everybody knew about it because the newspapers published reports of what happened to them. They were all rejected, but we weren't. I don't know why. Maybe the ship or the alien has learned a lesson or something and now he's trying a different approach by letting me find the right replacement."

"I see. God, this is weird. So, who's going to do the actual probing and whatever? Is the ship delegating that to you too?"

"Hmm, I honestly don't know. As I mentioned last time we met, I'm pretty good with cows and other animals if I really have to be, but I expect probing a human might be quite different. I have faith the ship will tell me what to do if it is me."

Harlan fell silent for several long moments again, before glancing down at the time on his cell phone.

"Okay, look Arthur. My lunch break is almost over and I have to head back to work soon. Time to get down to business, so here's the thing. I'm still not convinced this isn't some completely weird pipe dream or that I've somehow slipped into an alternate universe. Who knows? Maybe I've suffered a nervous breakdown and I'm in a loony bin somewhere having hallucinations because of whatever meds they're injecting into my body."

"I understand. It took time for my wife and I to come to understand and get used to what happened to us, too."

"I expect. So I need proof. See, I have to be able to convince myself this isn't any of that stuff I just mentioned. This means I also have to convince my friends, who are the toughest audience I know, that this is all really happening. I need a reality check on my sanity, right? And in particular, somewhere along the way you mentioned you figure I need a woman to join me, right? Well, I have someone in mind, but she's going to take the most convincing of all. I..."

Harlan paused for a long moment as he considered the utter weirdness of what exactly he had said.

"God, this is getting out of control," he said, shaking his head in disbelief. He took a moment to gather himself together and carried on.

"Look, Arthur. My friends are total sceptics. I need you to do something big to convince them this isn't a pile of crap. I don't know what 'big' means, but the ball is in your court for that. And they are going to want to meet you. If I tell them I've been talking to a guy who claims to live on a flying saucer, they will need some serious convincing I haven't completely lost my mind. In other words, I need a little help here, please? You know, do a fly past in your saucer or something. Come and probe somebody. God, I don't know."

"Sure, I understand. Look, why don't you have a long talk with your friends to start? Explain what you've seen and heard. If they want to meet me that's fine. I suggest we meet here in the park two days from now on your lunch break again. That will give you a couple of days to contact them and hopefully they can arrange their schedules to be there too. I'll show up here a little early to meet you in case you have questions or need to tell me anything before they arrive. How does that sound?"

"Uh, let's do it right after work instead. That will be Friday. It'll be way easier for them to coordinate being there. But why the park? How about doing it at The Lamp? We would all be there anyway around five o'clock."

"How about I meet you maybe fifteen minutes or so before that? And yes, it really should be the park. You want me to do something to prove myself, right? Not sure if you want me doing it in a real public spot like that nice old diner you go to."

"Hmm, good point. Okay, I can likely talk them into meeting in the park. The Lamp isn't all that far from here anyway. So don't keep me in suspense. What are you going to do to convince them?"

The old man smiled. "Well, as you said you need a little convincing yourself, so at some point when I meet them I'm going to do what I intend to do right now for you. See you Friday, Harlan."

A bare millisecond after the old man finished speaking, he simply vanished.

Harlan's brain needed a long moment to process the bizarre fact he was gone. Harlan shook his head in disbelief, rising from his seat to look about in all directions. He called out the old man's name several times as he did. His mind still refused to believe what he saw, but he couldn't dispute the fact the old man somehow managed to simply blink out of sight in an instant.

Despite himself, Harlan looked under the picnic table where he was sitting, but found nothing. Harlan even went over to search the nearest set of low bushes to see if Arthur was playing some sort of magic trick on him and was now hiding nearby, but he found nothing.

Walking back to the picnic table, he pulled out his phone to check the time and saw he needed to head back to the office. Harlan grabbed his lunch bag and shook his head one more time. He muttered to himself as he began to make his way out of the park.

"Good God, am I losing my mind? Sure hope not."

He reached the edge of the park and was waiting for the traffic light to change at the street corner when he a strange feeling came that he needed to look over his shoulder back to the picnic table. He took a moment to ask himself if he really wanted to do that, before finally succumbing to the temptation.

When he did, it strangely seemed logical to see the same mysterious van was now parked on the street as close as possible to the same picnic table where Harlan was sitting only minutes before with Arthur. Two men wearing ball caps and sunglasses were stalking rapidly about the area, checking every patch of brush nearby, as if in search for something they obviously weren't finding. Harlan put his hand to his forehead and groaned, before forcing himself to turn away and carry on back to the office.

***

As he left the office at the end of the day his mind was still in as much of a fog as it was when going back to work after lunch in the park. He knew tomorrow morning he would have to double check everything he did at work that afternoon, for not being totally focused on the work he was doing at all times was always a recipe for disaster. Halfway to his apartment he was still lost in the fog and, after realizing he couldn't face making dinner, he detoured to a nearby restaurant for take-out.

Harlan paid for his food and stepped outside to wait in the fresh air while it was being cooked, for the restaurant was stuffy and warm. Despite the murk still inside his brain he gradually sensed a few minutes later that he was once again being watched, and he swung his head back and forth to study the street. He was unsurprised to find the mystery black van parked nearby, a half block away. Losing patience with yet more weirdness in his life, Harlan stalked down the sidewalk toward the van.

As he got within a short distance from the rear of the van the engine started with a roar and it hurriedly backed up in the parking stall to pull out into traffic. Harlan sprinted the last few feet to the driver's side door in time to see the same two men inside. Neither acknowledged Harlan, who shouted at them as he stood on the sidewalk with arms wide in open question.

"What? I'm here. What do you want with me? Come on!"

As he finished speaking the van pulled out and sped away, Harlan walked out into the street to stand there waving his arms at them in frustration. After a car honked its horn at him Harlan finally turned his attention away from the van and went back to the sidewalk, only now realizing exactly how busy the street was with people going home. Several people on the sidewalk were slowly backing away from him and displaying wary, questioning looks on their faces. Harlan focused on the nearest of them, a young man and woman who obviously just picked up their own take-out food from a different restaurant for themselves.

"Uh...look, these bastards have been following me everywhere and I don't know why," said Harlan, as he pointed down the street before finally realizing how crazy that sounded. "I...God, never mind."

The man kept the wary look on his face as he shoved the bag of food he was carrying into his girlfriend's hands and steered her behind him with one hand, while continuing to back further away. He put forward his other hand as if to hold Harlan back and he replied using a deliberately soothing tone of voice.

"Sure man. Whatever you say."

Harlan made to speak again, but he shook his head as he changed his mind. He turned away and started walking back to the restaurant where he saw one of the servers standing outside the front door with his own bag of take-out food in her hand. As Harlan walked up he saw she too was wearing a guarded look on her face and he surmised she saw the whole encounter with the van. Instead of waiting for him to get close she put the bag on the ground, pointed to it, and beat a fast retreat back into the restaurant.

The rest of the way home Harlan was completely preoccupied by trying to figure out how exactly he was going to explain this to his friends. After wolfing down his dinner he slumped into his desk chair and powered up his computer, opening a fresh email to compose and send. But the blank email screen stayed that way, despite several attempts to start. Each time he did, the words didn't seem right, so he deleted them to start again. The struggle was over how much detail to provide.

After getting up and walking about in frustration for a few minutes Harlan finally groaned, forcing himself to sit down and simply start typing. Ten minutes later a draft was ready to go. While still unsatisfied and certain everyone reading it would question his sanity, he knew it wasn't going to get better. In the end he decided to keep his message simple, leaving room for them to come with questions if they weren't going to dismiss him outright.

With a flash of insight Harlan slapped his forehead, frustrated by how he easily he overlooked the one piece of solid evidence he already had in his possession to use. Within moments he pulled up the photo he took the day before of the mysterious van and attached it to the email to send to his friends. While far from conclusive, he was sure the van's exterior appearance was strange enough that even the most sceptical of his friends would acknowledge it was definitely unusual.

After doing a bit more basic editing he sat back

to do one final read through of the message. As he did, Spock landed on the desk with a thud and let out a loud meow to announce his presence. Harlan grabbed him, pulling him into his arms a millisecond before the cat was about to flop on the keyboard.

"No, you don't, you little bugger. Not this time, Spock."

If a cat could appear aggrieved, Harlan was certain the look on Spock's face was what it would look like. Harlan could have sworn the second meow that followed the first also carried an offended edge to it, too. Harlan sighed.

"Look, you are not sending the email this time. I am."

Reaching out Harlan tapped the enter key and the email disappeared from his screen.

"Happy now? I expect a treat will make you even happier."

After feeding Spock a couple of treats, which did indeed seem to placate the animal, Harlan shut down his computer and stood up.

"God, I need a beer. Come on, Spock, let's go see if your owner is outside."

As Harlan picked up Spock and stepped outside, he was unsurprised to see Isaac sitting alone on his deck, a beer in hand. His neighbour looked over on hearing Harlan come out.

"Ah, there he is. I figured he might be over bothering you again."

"He's no bother, Isaac. He's actually a welcome distraction from my bizarre day," replied Harlan, as he put Spock down. "I'll be right back. I really need a beer."

On his return Harlan made his way straight over to the Isaac's deck and slumped into one of his chairs. Spock was already sitting on the old man's lap, purring madly.

"A bizarre day, you say? Sounds intriguing. More to do with your alleged alien, I assume? Do tell."

Harlan took a large pull at his beer and nodded. When he finished telling the story five minutes later he looked at his glass and realized over three quarters of his drink was already gone. He looked over at Isaac to gauge his reaction. The old man sat in silence the whole time, wearing an expressionless face until now. He reached up to rub in chin in obvious thought, before finally grunting softly.

"Huh. He's here to make sure humans don't blow themselves back to the stone age, eh? Well, that's interesting, isn't it, Spock?"

The cat looked up at Isaac and gave a loud meow in response. Harlan gave Isaac a puzzled look.

"Uh, dumb question, but why would Spock find that interesting?"

"Oh, don't mind me, Harlan," said Isaac with a laugh. "Sorry, force of habit from living alone with a cat. After a while you start talking to him as if he was human, too. No, I'm just a little surprised this is what your farmer's job is. I wasn't expecting that one, that's for sure."

Harlan was silent for a moment before giving a mental shrug and downing the remnants of his drink.

"Well, neither was I. Anyway, I'm going to make

this an early night. If I stay out here longer I'll be tempted to get more beer, so I'd have the option of pretending this was all just some drunken fantasy. I'm better off going to bed, because I'm going to have a long day tomorrow explaining this to my friends."

And as Harlan trudged back into his apartment, he never saw the mystery van slowly cruise by on the street outside once again.

Chapter Seven

Harlan knew the easiest and most central place for everyone to meet was The Lamp, so that was the location he suggested they get together for lunch. He was sure questions were inevitably in their minds. After talking to both Keiko and Jordi briefly at work he knew at least they were planning to be there. He was a bit dismayed to find he was the first to arrive, but one by one everyone appeared. Carrie showed up and took food orders, but no one ordered beer as it would make for a long afternoon back at work. As Carrie walked away Harlan couldn't take the suspense any longer and looked around the table.

"Right, let's get on with it. Come on, everyone. Tell me I'm insane."

"The guy disappeared, huh?" said Jordi. "Have to confess that's a bit on the weird, but mundane side. I figured he'd get out some kind of blaster and vaporize a tree or something. Maybe turn you into a toad and then turn you back to yourself again. Got to be the good stuff you've been smoking lately, huh?"

"Well, of course he'd disappear, Jordi," said Clifford. "If he has alien technology why wouldn't he be able to do that? Has to be able to hide when he needs to. And even more impressive, Harlan has government agents following him around now. Damn, Harlan, I was going to come over and have a look at your telescope, but this is way better. I'll be there tomorrow for the meeting for sure."

"Not sure I buy your logic, Clifford," said

Spider. "But I too am unsurprised. Go read any science fiction story and you'll usually find they involve aliens having some kind of stealth capability. If they didn't, we would have found them by now, wouldn't we? So assuming Harlan hasn't completely lost his mind, I for one am prepared to buy it as well. Naturally, this is a rather large assumption. Harlan looks and acts perfectly normal, doesn't he? I shall keep a little bit of scepticism nonetheless."

"Of course you lunatics would all believe it, wouldn't you?" said Keiko. "I, for one, would like to introduce a big dose of that scepticism. I need to see something for myself. Sorry, Harlan."

"No need to apologize. I needed to be convinced myself."

"But let me get this straight, Harlan," said Deanna. "You say you have these guys following you around, right? And you think they must be government spies or something?"

"Well, I don't know who else they could be. They have this van with all these weird antennas on it and they certainly are persistent. I mean, you all saw the picture I attached, right?"

"Yeah, it's a weird looking van, but that's about all I can concede, Harlan. But let's move on. I'm thinking this is where we all get sucked in, right?" said Nyota. "You're going to want us to be wearing tinfoil hats when we meet with this farmer of yours, is that it?"

Harlan sighed. "No, I never suggested that, but the way this is going I won't be surprised if some of you show up with them."

"Well, what I find amusing about all of this is the fact your farmer thinks you need a wife," said Keiko. "Who do you have in mind? I sure hope you aren't planning to suggest me."

"Hey, I get it now," said Jordi. "This is all just a plot to get into Keiko's bed. Have to admit, I admire your creativity. But Keiko doesn't sound like she's ready for that idea just yet. Hey, Keiko, how do you feel about getting probed anyway? Forget about aliens having their way with you, I'm quite sure I could do better."

"I'm sure you think so, but you are dreaming again, Jordi."

"For the record, Keiko, I have not suggested to the farmer that you join me."

"Not yet," said Jordi. "He wants you all to himself, Keiko. I'll bet if he tells the farmer you're the one, you'll find yourself getting beamed into this flying saucer whether you like it or not."

"Jordi, no one is going to be made to do anything. If I somehow end up on a flying saucer...God, I can't believe I'm saying that...Keiko won't be joining me unless she wants to," said Harlan, with a weary tone in his voice.

"Give it up, you two lunatics," said Keiko, rolling her eyes.

"Well, maybe if Harlan needs company someone else can join him. I'd consider it. It would be a perfect opportunity to learn more about exactly what the aliens have been doing," said Clifford.

"Assuming I'd want to spend the rest of forever trapped on an alien flying saucer with you is a big stretch, Clifford."

"Okay, I get it. Maybe we can just come and visit for a bit. Or why not take all of us? That would be cool, don't you think? As long as there's beer it would all be fine. We're all good friends. Besides, maybe alien beer will be better than the stuff we make on earth."

"Some of us like to drink wine, Clifford," said Deanna.

"The possibilities could be endless."

"Hmm, well, we'll maybe see. Harlan? There is one thing about this I find interesting in particular."

"And that is?"

"Why it would be your farmer's job to make sure we don't go boom and blow ourselves up. I mean, I guess it's good they want us around, but for what? I'd like to think they want to help us grow as a species, which heaven knows we need to do. It just seems weird to apparently have the wherewithal to save us from disaster, but to do it only if they must."

"Maybe they are just ensuring we don't wipe out humanity before they come along and eat us," said Jordi.

"Yes, I was wondering that, too. Make sure we've all grown as nice and fat and tasty as possible," said Clifford.

"My God, aren't you two a pair of cynics," said Deanna.

As their lunches arrived everyone fell to eating in silence. A few of them looked at their phones for the time and wolfed down the remainder of their food. Harlan signalled for their bills, knowing they all needed to get back to work. As they all finished paying Harlan looked around the table.

"Right, any more questions before we all get out of here?"

Everyone shook their heads so he continued.

"Well, I hope at least some of you will show up tomorrow. I'm meeting him in the park again right after work."

Clifford and Spider acknowledged they would be there, but coming for their usual Friday night dinner at The Lamp was all the rest of them would commit to. On seeing the crestfallen look on Harlan's face a few of them relented and agreed to be there too, which made the holdouts finally all agree to meet.

Harlan was privately pessimistic about the possibility of everyone showing up as he walked back to the office with Jordi and Keiko. After Jordi broke away to head for his workstation Harlan stopped Keiko from doing the same. She peered at him quizzically, sensing he wanted something.

"Keiko? I don't know about you, but I've got nothing to eat in my fridge. Haven't gotten my act together to do some grocery shopping. Feel like joining me at The Lamp for dinner tonight?"

A wary look briefly replaced the question written on her face, before she ducked her head as she tried to hide the rueful smile which Harlan wasn't expecting to see. She remained silent long enough Harlan finally spoke up.

"What? Have I said something amusing?"

"Sort of. By coincidence I am suffering with the same issue. I hadn't figured out what to do about it yet. Going to The Lamp is a decent solution, but I'm wondering if you really are going to ask me to join you on a flying saucer afterwards. So is that the plan?"

"What do you think? Of course not. Even if this all really is true and this farmer wants me on his spaceship, I can't imagine why I would want to do that. I suppose being able to zip off real quick to Greece for some real Greek food whenever I want might be cool, but I need a bit more convincing."

Harlan paused a moment, putting a hand to his forehead before continuing.

"Sorry, you don't get the reference. Arthur and his wife like Greek food. Anyway, as for you, well, there are no plans to have the alien or his space farmer to beam you up to the ship where I've got you all to myself."

"But you do want me all to yourself, don't you?"

Harlan spread his hands wide. "Haven't I made that clear?"

Keiko remained silent for a long moment before she shrugged and nodded.

"Sure, why not? I'll join you for dinner, because I need to eat something. The Lamp is as good as it gets and the price is right. I'll have to meet you there, though. Got to detour home to feed my cat. At least she's got some food for her in the apartment, unlike me."

Harlan smiled. "I'm heading to The Lamp right after work. I'll see you when you get there."

***

Carrie smiled when Harlan walked in and she came over to greet him.

"Well, I wasn't expecting you tonight. You're getting to be one of the most regular customers we have, even more than the others. Anyone else joining you?"

"Just Keiko, so all I need is a table for two, please. She is making a detour to her apartment, but she'll be here in a while. We'll be having dinner."

Carrie grinned. "Well. Things are looking up, I hope. She's a pretty woman. Might as well shoot for the stars. Why don't you take one of the view tables over by the big window? Make it a memorable night. Drink?"

"Yes, I'll have a beer and let's not get too enthusiastic about this just yet. One step at a time. And by the way, don't let me order another beer. You're right, I'm getting to be too good a customer and it's too easy to keep ordering more. The usual, please."

"Suit yourself. But if things really are looking up, I'd recommend some place a little classier than this. You know, a nice pasta joint with an expensive bottle of wine or something. Buy her some flowers and chocolates while you're at it. I've yet to meet a woman that can resist them. I know I can't. Meanwhile, beer it is."

Harlan was left smiling and shaking his head as she walked away, before pulling out his phone to check his messages and email. A pint of beer soon appeared in front of him, but this time Carrie said nothing and he didn't look up from his phone to encourage her.

He was still head down, surfing through his phone a minute later when as before he sensed someone sliding into the booth across the table from him. When a second person unexpectedly joined the first filling the bench seat opposite, he realized instantly his assumption it was Keiko was wrong. A premonition came that he was finally going to learn more about the mysterious men following him.

Harlan looked up to find he was correct. The two men, one black and one white, were both dressed in much the same way as the last time he saw them in the distance. Both wore sunglasses and ball caps with no logos on them. Their clothes were nondescript enough they could easily be considered acceptable for a casual business meeting or an afternoon at a baseball game.

Harlan looked back and forth at the two men, who seemed to be staring at him as if he were a bug under a microscope. Feeling frustrated at being hounded about by the pair, he resisted the urge to scowl as he waited for them to speak. They seemed in no rush to do so. Harlan let an edge creep into his voice as he took the initiative.

"Well? What do you want?"

The two men looked at each other briefly, before the white man turned back and spoke.

"We are here to talk to you, Harlan. We have a few questions we'd like to ask."

"Questions? Really. Okay, but first I have some questions for you. How exactly is it that you know my name? And who are you?"

"Oh, we know all about you, Harlan. We work for the government. If you must have names you can call me Larry. My partner here you can call...Ray. Our names are irrelevant."

"Fascinating. You claim to work for the government and are giving me some fake names. Come on, gentlemen. If you want me to believe this nonsense then let's get past this 'irrelevant' notion and show me your identification."

"We have identification, but we can't show it to you," said the black man named Ray. "Security reasons. I'm sure you understand."

Harlan rolled his eyes. "No, I don't bloody understand. Hey, if you guys are some kind of super spooks for the government or whatever why aren't you wearing suits? I thought that was a given."

"Only in the movies, sir. Suits don't really serve our purposes anymore."

"Oh, I get it. You two are being more subtle about it. Casual clothes for both of you. And the sunglasses and ball caps with no identifiers on them. So if someone takes a photo of you it would be hard to make out distinguishing features, right? Facial recognition and all that. Damn, maybe you two are spooks after all. Why don't you cut the crap and at least lose the shades. You couldn't stand out more if you were a pair of unicorns."

The two men looked at each other once again and neither spoke. After a quick look in all directions to see who was watching them, as one they took off the sunglasses. Sensing his message hit the mark, Harlan used their silence to keep after them.

"Actually, I'll go one step further. You drive around in a van with all sorts of weird antennas and you work for the government. I'll bet you two work at Area 51, don't you? Maybe you're looking for aliens trying to take over the country or the world. Damn, that could be an interesting job. Are you taking applications? I've been thinking about a career change lately. Or wait, maybe you're actually the aliens and you're just messing with my mind! The possibilities are endless, aren't they?"

"We can't confirm or deny anything about Area 51, sir, and even if we did know something we wouldn't be talking to you about it, now would we?" said Larry. "I..."

He was interrupted by the appearance of Carrie standing beside the table with her order pad out.

"Gentlemen, you're back again. Can I get you anything?"

"No. Please go away, we need to speak to this man alone."

Carrie frowned at the cold dismissal in his voice, but made no move to leave.

"You know, we have bills to pay here at The Lamp. Most people that come in here help us with that."

The man named Larry rolled his eyes. "Fine. Bring us two cups of coffee and leave us, thank you."

"Coming right up," said Carrie, offering Harlan a surreptitious look of annoyance which made it clear what she thought of the two men.

Harlan used the distraction she offered to go back on the offensive with the two men.

"Look gentlemen. You follow me around in a weird van, you finally show up here acting and dressing like you've got something to hide, and you claim to be working for the government, although you aren't prepared to prove that. If you want my cooperation with whatever you are after, you are going to have to do better. You need to tell me what this is about and what your role is in it all."

"Sir," said Ray. "Give us a chance to tell you more. We realize this likely seems highly unusual. Please understand we are not here to do something nefarious to you. We are just...communications specialists. That's the best we can offer to tell you. As for what this is all about, it may well be something important enough to have big and serious implications for national security. Or maybe not. This is why we have to talk to you, to find out more. We have a mystery on our hands and we really do need your help. In particular, we..."

Once again Carrie appeared and the two men ceased talking as she dropped two cups of coffee on the table in front of them.

"Two coffees, as requested. Flag me down if you need anything else."

As she walked away this time it was Larry that spoke up.

"Look, we have a few questions for you. Have you had anything unusual happen to you lately, sir?"

Harlan raised an eyebrow, unable to stop from allowing a smile to appear on his face.

"Aside from you two following me around, I assume you mean?"

"Sir, we are serious," said Ray. "And yes, aside from us. For instance, I can't help but notice you mentioned Area 51 and aliens a while back. Any reason that came to mind?"

Harlan was silent for a few long moments before he responded.

"Of course there's a reason. I expect the two of

you know more about it that I do. You aren't interested in me, are you? You are interested in the old man."

The two agents looked at each other once again, before turning back to Harlan. The agent named Larry sighed and spoke, a hint of frustration in his voice.

"Look Harlan. We know you've seen the wobble up there. We also know you've talked to the old man. This guy."

Pulling an old, grainy photograph out of an inside pocket of his coat he held it out for Harlan to inspect. The photo was worn at the edges and showed its age, but he was certain was indeed a photo of Arthur, despite how blurred and grainy it was. He appeared to be looking over his shoulder at the camera, which was obviously some distance away from him. Harlan realized after a moment studying it that Arthur seemed a bit younger in this photograph.

"Well, at least we're getting somewhere now. See, I was right. You two do know more than you are letting on. So, first question for you. How exactly is it you know I've seen the wobble you refer to?"

Larry sighed. "Look, we know you aren't particularly dense, Harlan. How do you think we know that? Of course we are reading your email and texts. We are communications specialists and we have the tools to do that, right? So we just want to know more. Who is he, what does he want, and, most importantly, why does he want it?"

Harlan rubbed his chin and nodded. "All right,

point taken. But this still isn't making sense yet. If you really are so all powerful, as I would expect the government to be, what are you asking me all this for?"

"I don't follow you."

"You're following me around. You claim to have special tools and you know I've been talking to him. Of course you have the wherewithal to pick up and listen to our conversations from a distance. At least I assume you do. So why are you asking me all these questions?"

Larry grimaced and cleared his throat, clearly buying himself time to make a decision, before he finally sighed.

"We do have the kind of tools you refer to, obviously. The problem is something is jamming our reception when he is around and we don't know what it is. It isn't just we can't listen in to conversations, we can't even get photos or video of him and we haven't figured out how to defeat it. We keep trying, of course. We don't know if it is deliberate, but we assume it likely is. So this old photo we got a hold of years ago is all we have. This is the truth, Harlan. So as painful as it is to admit this, we really are in the dark."

Harlan frowned. "Wait a minute. So let me understand, you are monitoring my conversations with him, but you are being jammed. I've been talking to my friends about him when he isn't around. So why don't you know what I've told them?"

"Good question, we would like to know that too. The real strange part of this is your conversations with anyone, and not just the old man, seem to be getting jammed, too. Trust me, we have tested this on other people. Some predecessors of ours got lucky years ago just to be able to get that photo of him. We haven't been able to manage it since. Our equipment works fine as long as you or this old man aren't around."

The agent paused a moment, allowing a pleading look to appear on his face.

"Look, Harlan, this is important. Your government needs your help. As we told you, this may have serious implications for national security. Or not. We don't know until we have the facts. Yes, we can read your emails and we know you say he disappeared on you yesterday. Bits of information like that spawn dozens of questions. We need much, much more than this. So your willing cooperation to fill in our knowledge gaps would be very, very helpful."

From the corner of his eye Harlan saw a familiar movement outside and turning to look he saw Keiko was now making her way down the street toward The Lamp. He turned back to the two agents.

"Gentlemen, I am here because I am being joined by a friend for dinner and she will be here shortly. I will be honest with you both, I am of two minds about all of this. Can I have some time to think about this?"

The two men looked at each other before Larry responded.

"We will check back with you. If you are prepared to cooperate with us we could certainly make it worth your while. We strongly suggest you do so. It is your choice not to cooperate, of course, but I really think it would be far better for you if you did."

"What does that mean? Is that a threat?"

Larry shrugged. "Not a threat, but you're going to choose to think of it however you want. We just believe it would be a really good idea to be our friend. Enjoy your dinner, sir. We will be in touch."

The two men put their sunglasses back on as they slid out of the booth. Larry pulled out his wallet and threw a bill on the table to pay for the coffees, before they both made for the door in silence. Keiko was walking in as they reached it and she stopped on seeing them, blocking the doorway. Harlan knew the puzzled look on her face was due to the sunglasses and their attire, which was all out of place for The Lamp. As she realized she was blocking the door, all three of them jockeyed around to get out of each other's way.

"Excuse us, ma'am," said Ray, as the two agents finally left.

Keiko remained watching them for a long moment, the puzzled look still on her face. She finally shook her head and turning, came over to join Harlan. She raised an eyebrow as she slipped into the booth.

"Huh. That was weird. Don't see people wearing sunglasses indoors every day."

"It was weirder than you think. They are the guys that have been following me in this strange van and they were here to talk to me. They claim to be government agents."

"Really?" said Keiko, unable to keep an obvious

look of scepticism off her face.

The look stayed there as Harlan told her about the conversation. As he finished he could tell she remained unconvinced, but before she could speak Carrie appeared at the table. She looked curiously at the two of them before sliding a couple of menus across the table.

"Hi, Keiko. So Harlan, who are those guys?"

Harlan shrugged. "Darned if I know. They claim to be government agents. Chasing aliens, I think. If that makes any sense."

"That wouldn't surprise me. They sure seemed like cops to me. They asked enough bloody questions."

"What do you mean?" said Keiko, the puzzled look appearing on her face again. "You've talked to them too?"

"Sure. Remember that day you met the old guy with his shirt on inside out, Harlan? After you left, the old man hung around for a bit and then he disappeared. And I mean he seems to have literally disappeared. One minute he was there and the next he wasn't. And right after that those two showed up and started asking a ton of questions. Wouldn't answer any themselves. So this old guy is an alien, is he?"

"He claims he isn't. Says he's a farmer, but he lives on a flying saucer."

"Huh. You know, I've watched a lot of interesting shit happen over the years in The Lamp, but this is taking it to a whole new level. Nothing a beer can't fix. Can I bring you two a drink?"

Both Harlan and Keiko gave her their orders.

Carrie smiled as she turned to leave.

"Coming right up. And Harlan? Do me a favour, please. Make sure none of these crazies don't pull out a ray gun and start vaporizing people."

They watched her walk away in silence before turning to look at each other as one. Harlan remained deliberately silent, waiting for Keiko to speak. He could see the confusion written on her face and she made to say something a couple of times, but stopped in doubt. Harlan held up his hands and shrugged.

"It's like I've been telling all of you. This shit is real, as bizarre as it may be. So tell me, are you starting to believe I'm not a lunatic after all?"

"I...I, well, maybe. I suppose I should tell you I noticed the van outside. I recognized it from the picture you sent. You're right, it looks as weird as those two. I...crap, I need some time to digest this."

"You and me both. That's why I told them I needed some time to think about it."

"So you didn't tell them much of anything, right? You don't trust them?"

"No, I didn't tell them much. Trust them? Hmm, might take some effort for that. You know, a lot of people don't trust the government, but I'm not one of them. Most government jobs are thankless and the people doing them are just trying to do the best they can, right? But these guys? Yeah, well, I'll keep an open mind, but they need to do better."

"What will you do?"

"Good question. Since my farmer friend seems to be well aware of them, as he is allegedly somehow jamming their communications, maybe he's the one that can give me some answers. Yeah, that's an idea. I think I'll see if I can have a little chat about this with my new friend Arthur before we meet everyone else tomorrow."

Chapter Eight

Harlan left work a little early at the end of the day Friday to make his way to the park. On arriving he made his way to the same area filled with picnic tables he'd met Arthur at before. As usual there were very few people in the area. He found no sign of Arthur when he arrived, but he was confident that would change soon enough. Moments after Harlan sat down Arthur appeared at his side, moving to sit at the table across from him.

"Thanks for coming, Harlan. You're early. Are your friends coming too?"

"Oh, they'll be here. Listen, the reason I came a bit early is I wanted to talk to you about some guys that have been following me ever since you appeared on the scene. I was trying to ignore them as being just more of the weirdness going on, but they finally came forward to talk to me. They claim to be government agents. They aren't interested in me, of course. They want to know about you. Of even more interest, their story is you are somehow jamming their equipment so they can't listen in or take pictures of you. Mind you, they actually do have what looks like a real old photo of you. Do you know anything about them?"

Arthur smiled. "Sure. They really do work for the government. Sorry, I suppose I should have mentioned they might find you."

"Hmm. So what they are saying is true?"

"Well, that's what the ship tells me. Yes, they saw the wobble a long time ago, just like you did. They managed to get a picture of me a long time ago because back then the ship and I were still new to this. I wasn't as careful about when and where I appear, you see. I made the rookie mistake of appearing seemingly from nowhere in a large crowd. Several people saw me and, as it happened, one of them was an amateur photographer with his camera handy. He alerted the government about the whole incident and showed them the photo. It took them a while, but once they realized he wasn't a lunatic, they confiscated it and gave him a large pile of money to keep his mouth shut. I'm sure they were puzzled as hell about what was going on, but some bright, educated youngster obviously made the connection between my appearance and the strange wobble in orbit. They had no other explanation. They've been watching close ever since."

"I expect. And you actually are jamming their communications somehow?"

"The ship is. I learned to rely on the ship for a lot of things. It's amazing, really. I just pose a problem for it and ask for a solution. It hasn't let me down yet. So given I've been having conversations with you, I asked the ship a while back to extend its jamming, as you call it, to you as well."

"Well, that explains why they mentioned they were having problems listening to me, too. Arthur, they've been really persistent following me. I didn't see them on my way here, but I wouldn't be surprised if they'll find me soon enough. I don't know, maybe they've planted some sort of tracking device on me. What do you want to do about them?"

Arthur was silent for a moment, staring into the

distance at nothing. After a long moment he refocused on Harlan.

"The ship says they aren't in the area. At least, not yet. It will monitor for their presence. I'll know if they are going to make an appearance. As for doing something about them, I'm not real concerned. A bunch of other governments around the world have known about the wobble for years, too. They keep steering satellites my direction to try and get close up pictures and what not, but the ship simply deflects them away while jamming anything they try to do. A couple of them even tried to blow me up with missiles, but the ship just sends them off into deep space where they destruct harmlessly. The last couple of times someone tried using some of these new-fangled, high-powered lasers, but that got them nowhere too."

"Wow. But I guess I can understand why they might be persistent."

Arthur shrugged. "I don't have a problem with governments. They are just doing what they think they are supposed to. The only real issue is I'm not too sure they would be positive about any of this were I allowed to reveal myself to them. I mean, seriously, even I know this ship has powers beyond anything we have on earth. I'd like to think a government given access to that kind of power would do good things with it, but my less optimistic side knows at least some of the people in charge in some countries would be tempted to do some real bad things."

"Yes, I'd share your concern about that. But can't you just have the ship make them forget they even saw the wobble or the photo of you?"

"Don't think so. I actually posed that notion to the ship a long time ago, but the answer was no. I truly don't know why not."

Harlan waved as he saw several of his friends come into the clearing and head over to join them.

"Hmm. Arthur, some of my friends are here to join us. So I have one other question for you while we are waiting, purely out of curiosity. I asked these two guys from the government about Area 51 and they wouldn't give me a straight answer about whether they were connected with it or not. Do you know anything about it? Have they got other aliens there or an alien ship of some sort?"

"Oh, an excellent question, Harlan. I'd like to know the answer to that, too," said Clifford as he slipped into the seat beside Harlan, an excited look on his face. "I assume this is your man that lives in the saucer. Well, please don't keep us in suspense."

As more of his friends came up to join them Harlan groaned, frowning at Clifford.

"At least give me a moment to introduce you all, Clifford."

Clifford sat squirming with barely contained impatience while Harlan did that. When Harlan finished Clifford dove right back into the conversation.

"Okay, fine, that's done. Now what was this about government agents? Are they really from Area 51? Have they got an alien ship there?"

"God, Clifford, give the man a chance, why don't you?" said Nyota, before turning to look at Arthur. "We should apologize. He's a little intense about this stuff sometimes."

"It's not a problem, but thank you for your consideration. I don't let much faze me anymore. After living for well over sixty years on a flying saucer, it would take a lot to do that. Anyway, I am sorry, but I can't help you with that. I've heard of this place, of course. Who hasn't? But I've never had cause to ask the ship about it. I wouldn't be surprised if these people following you were connected to this place, though. I suppose I could do that if you really want to know. And another alien ship? I doubt it, but I've learned not to discount anything."

"Okay, hang on a minute," said Jordi, a puzzled look on his face. "What is this about government agents? Are you telling me this weird van he sent a picture of actually is filled with a bunch of spooks?"

"We haven't had a chance to tell you about what happened yesterday," said Keiko. "I met them. Harlan, tell everyone so we are all on the same page."

Harlan gave them the details of his meeting with the agents the day before, adding Arthur's explanation that the ship was in fact actively jamming conversations involving both Arthur and Harlan. He also explained what Arthur told him about the lack of success governments around the world suffered over the years. After he finished a long moment of silence ensued as everyone processed what he said. Deanna finally broke it as she stared at Arthur, wearing a puzzled look on her face as she spoke.

"Something is weird here. I can't put my finger

on it."

Spider shuffled in his seat, obviously watching her and waiting his turn to speak while deferring to Deanna. When she didn't continue, he turned to Arthur.

"Yes, well, there is lots of weird going on here. Sir, I have a few questions for you, if you don't mind."

"Yeah, I got some too," said Jordi. "Like, can you show us an alien death ray or something? How about whatever device you have that hides you and the ship? Maybe some alien food. You know, something with lots of icky tentacles."

"Jordi, get serious," said Spider.

"No, no, it's okay," said Arthur. "I expected some disbelief. But I'm afraid I don't have a death ray. I haven't seen anything like that on the ship. As for whatever hides me and the ship, well, that would be the ship itself. And food? I have no idea what aliens eat. I certainly haven't seen any tentacles anywhere on the ship. Me, I like pizza. The wife and I get takeout all the time. I can recommend some great places if you're interested."

"Right, well, I have some serious questions for you," said Spider, glaring at Jordi for a moment. "So let me get this straight. So according to Harlan you say you're supposed to make sure the world doesn't blow itself up. Why is that? I mean, really, why would an alien care about that? Is there more to this, like maybe the universe needs saving or something?"

Arthur looked apologetic. "Well, you are right, I am supposed to keep an eye on things and make sure humans don't do something silly like destroy the world, but I have no idea why. As for the universe? Hmm, that's way beyond my job."

"Huh," said Spider. "So how exactly do you go about making sure we aren't about to do that?"

"Oh, my wife and I watch a lot of television. It helps pass the time and you'd be amazed how much you can learn."

"Okay, like, if I was some lunatic world leader with my finger on the trigger of a bunch of nukes, I'm not real likely to be going on the tube to tell the world I'm about to blow someone up. So I don't get how that works."

"Ah, sorry, I assumed you already understood the other part of this. The ship monitors all kinds of communications and warns me when someone is talking about doing bad things. This is how I found Harlan in the first place, because his email mentioned my coordinates. So I watch a whole bunch of tv and warn the ship about people I think warrant some extra attention. Teamwork, you see."

Arthur paused to give them an apologetic smile before continuing.

"I guess I should clarify, I'm the one that watches a lot of news programs to stay on top of it all. My wife watches soap operas."

"So you're saying you've done nothing but watch tv for the last sixty years?" said Nyota, wearing a look a disbelief on her face.

Arthur shrugged. "Well, if you have a job to do you might as well do it right. Like I told Harlan here, we do take little vacations to different places once in a while. We've been all over the world. I have to confess being on the saucer has certainly broadened our horizons."

"God, this is strange," said Deanna, still wearing a puzzled look on her face.

"So the government wants to get their hands on you badly, right?" said Clifford, ignoring Deanna. "With the resources they have, how is it possible they haven't succeeded?

"Hmm, well, it isn't for lack of trying. And speaking of which, I'm afraid they are trying once again. We may not have much longer before we are interrupted."

"Good God, is this going to get even weirder?" said Nyota.

"It's already weird," said Deanna, shaking her head in puzzlement.

"They are back?" said Harlan, turning and looking about.

The others followed suit, looking nervously over their shoulders as they tried to find the agents with their mysterious van. Spider was the one who finally noticed the odd sound in the background and looked up.

"Hey, look, that's a drone above us. I thought I heard something weird."

Everyone looked up and saw he was right. Hovering over one hundred feet above them was a small drone. The underside bore what appeared to be a camera which moved slightly from side to side as the drone shifted position in the sky above.

"How about that?" said Nyota, as she gazed skyward. "This really is getting weirder and that thing has a camera. Might as well wave and smile for the nice drone, people."

"Hey, I don't know where the van is, but I think I saw someone or something move in that bush over there," said Jordi, pointing to a spot on the far side of the clearing. "I wonder if he's the operator?"

"Huh. Let's go find out," said Clifford, an eager look on his face. "I'd like to meet an honest to God, real live government spook from Area 51. Who's with me?"

'I'm in," said Spider. "Let's go."

The two men stood up as one and raced across the clearing toward the bush Jordi pointed at. As they neared the spot the bushes rustled with movement, proving Jordi was right. Whoever was in them went the opposite direction in a hurry, leaving nothing in the brush for them to find. They were still searching in vain when Jordi called out again, loud enough for them to hear.

"Harlan? Is that your weird van over there? Hey guys, they're escaping!"

Both Clifford and Spider looked in the new direction Jordi was now pointing, where a dark van was now pulled up by the side of the road in the distance. Everyone realized at once it was the van with strange antennas, matching the photo of the one Harlan sent them all.

Clifford and Spider turned and began running toward it, as a white man burst from cover in the brush. He held a control device in his hands and was frantically trying to bring the drone to ground while he escaped. He looked over his shoulder and saw the two men still coming, distracting him enough to lose control of the machine. The drone crashed hard to the pavement beside the van, damaging it enough to break into two pieces. The man cursed and glared over his shoulder at Clifford and Spider, gathered up both halves of the drone, and jumped into the waiting van.

"Hey, hang on a minute. We'd like to talk to you!" shouted Clifford as they ran up, but the government agents were having none of it. The van's engine gunned to life and it sped off down the street, leaving the two men waving their arms and finally stumbling slowly to a halt.

A young woman with a baby in a stroller on the sidewalk a short distance away stopped in her tracks, watching as the whole tableau unfolded before her. As she watched, a mixed look of disbelief, shock, and uncertainty all materialized on her face. Spider noticed her and, on seeing the question in her eyes, gave her a sheepish grin as he pointed at the van disappearing down the street.

"Sorry we surprised you. They're government agents from Area 51. They've been following us around."

The woman's eyes widened and, without responding, she wheeled the stroller about, almost running to get away. Harlan came up as Spider made to call after her, but Clifford forestalled him.

"Yeah, I have that effect on women, too. Get used to it."

"So we saw what happened," said Harlan. "Out of curiosity, did either of you get a look at the driver?"

"Yeah, I did," said Clifford. "Why do you ask?"

"He was a black guy, right? Wearing a ball cap

and sunglasses?"

"Yes. How did you know?"

"Those are my government agents all right. Let's head back to the others."

As the three men walked back to the table Harlan peered about and realized Arthur was nowhere in sight. He gave the others a questioning look.

"When did Arthur leave?"

The others at the table looked around in surprise, only now realizing he was gone. Clifford and Spider poked their heads into the nearby brush to no avail and both men came back shaking their heads. Spider looked at Harlan as he asked the question the rest of them had on their minds.

"So? What happened to him, Harlan?"

Harlan shrugged. "He probably disappeared again as soon as those idiots following me showed up. He doesn't seem to like getting his picture taken. None of you saw him disappear, though, did you?"

"You haven't gotten around to asking him how he manages that, have you?" said Deanna.

"Not yet, but we're going to have to ask, aren't we?"

"So where do we go from here?" said Nyota. "I confess I need a little time to process this."

"I need more than a little time," said Keiko, holding her head in her hands. "Like maybe a decade or so? I can't decide if this is all some bizarre pipe dream or not. The one thing I do know is it's messing with my head."

"What?" said Jordi. "Not ready to get hitched and move into a flying saucer? I can't imagine why not."

"God," said Nyota. "Give it a rest, Jordi. I need a

drink. Keiko isn't the only one who thinks this is all beyond belief."

Several of them nodded agreement, with varying degrees of puzzlement still obvious on their faces. Clifford was the one who finally spoke up.

"Yes, we need to process this alright. And I can't think of a better way to do that than to head for The Lamp. It's Friday night and Carrie has a table ready for us. We can discuss this madness over an ocean of beer. Anyone with me?"

***

Harlan was a little unsteady from all the beer as he unlocked the entrance to his apartment and came in, fumbling with the light switch as he did. The night was warm so he slid the balcony door open to let in the slightly cooler night air. He heard a familiar meow and looked down to see Spock sitting in one of Harlan's deck chairs, with a hopeful look on his face.

"Waiting for a treat, are you?" said Harlan.

The sound of Isaac's exasperated voice came from next door a second later.

"Spock, you greedy little beast. Leave Harlan alone."

"That's okay, Isaac. I've kept him waiting for his treats tonight. I'll give him an extra one if that's okay. Just give me a minute, I'm a little under the weather here."

"Under the weather?"

"No more beer for me tonight. Need to sober up or the bed is going to spin on me."

"Ah. You can tell me about it while you do that. I've got some leftover pizza if you want to soak up some of the beer."

"Sounds like a fine idea. Come on, Spock. You know where I keep the treats."

"I'll microwave a couple of pieces and bring them out."

Two minutes later Harlan was finishing wolfing down the pizza as Isaac sat across from him with his usual beer in hand and Spock purring loudly in his lap. Isaac waited for him to finish before he spoke.

"Better?"

"Much. Overdid it a bit tonight. We all did."

"Any particular reason or just because it's Friday night?"

"Hmm, both are applicable, I think. Been a long, strange week."

"Well. I've got time to listen while you sober up."

Harlan eyed the beer in Isaac's hand, needing something to wash the pizza down, so he went to get a beer for himself. He poured half the bottle into a glass and gave the other half to Isaac as he began telling his neighbour everything. Isaac sat in silence for several long moments, rubbing his chin in thought, before he finally spoke.

"Yes, I'd say that qualifies as strange. So what are you going to do now? And what did your friends think about it all?"

Harlan sighed. "The reactions are all over the place. The range is from total disbelief, like it was all some weird collective mirage we experienced, to those who want to get probed and recruited by the alien or aliens right now. And every reaction in between. Of course, the fact it's been a long week and it's Friday night didn't help. Let's just say I'm not the only one who downed a few too many drinks tonight."

"I see. And now?"

"The only decision we came to was to get together tomorrow for lunch at The Lamp. By the end of the night that was the only reasonably sober thought any of us could manage. We can nurse our collective hangovers with a ton of coffee, but in honesty I think the only real decision, at least on their part, is whether any of them want to meet with Arthur again. There are a few disbelievers in the group, as I said."

"Ah. And one of them is the girl you are chasing, correct?"

"Sadly, yes, although I think she is more confused than anything else. And having said that, I am done. My bed is calling."

As both Harlan and Isaac rose from their seats Isaac pointed down the street.

"Out of curiosity, is that your government agent's van over there? The one with all the weird antennas?"

Harlan looked at where Isaac was pointing and scowled.

"Yes, it certainly is. Persistent bastards, I have to give them that. I'd go chase after them again, but I'm done with this for tonight. If those lunatics want to sit there all night and sleep in their clothes waiting for me to do something, then let them. I chase them in the morning after I've inhaled a pot of coffee."

Isaac picked up his beer and motioned to Spock,

who was lying on the ground at their feet.

"Yes, you do look a little worse for wear. See you tomorrow, perhaps. And Harlan? My advice is don't sweat it. I have a feeling this will all work out for the best. Come on, Spock. Harlan needs to go to bed."

"I hope so. Goodnight," said Harlan, turning and heading inside for the night.

***

Back on his own deck with Spock, Isaac made certain his neighbour really was gone to bed by waiting to ensure Harlan's lights were out for the night. Once he was sure, Isaac stood up and went to the edge of his patio, picking up Spock as he went. He peered out at the mystery van, still parked a little way down the street.

"Yes, Harlan is right, they are persistent, aren't they, Spock? I guess we should do something about this, wouldn't you agree?"

Isaac smiled at the cat, who jumped down from his arms and disappeared into the nearby bushes, heading in the direction of the van. Isaac remained standing in the shadows, staring intently down the street. After a couple of minutes he grunted and a smile appeared on his face. A few moments later he began to chuckle as noise of a commotion from the direction of the van reached him. The voices of men shouting ever louder began drawing attention from other people living on the street, as Isaac saw lights being turned on all around the area and windows being opened by curious inhabitants.

As the uproar grew even more raucous Isaac found himself almost doubled over, laughing out loud. The sound of men loudly cursing out on the street prompted some of the nearby residents to curse them in turn, telling them to shut up or they would call the police.

Moments later Spock reappeared, winding his way silently through the darkness of the nearby bushes. Once again the cat version of a grin was on his face as Isaac mastered himself and picked up his pet. Isaac scratched behind the cat's ears and Spock began to purr as Isaac took one last look down the street. A police car appeared on the scene and drove past, heading in the direction of the van.

"Well, that was amusing. Harlan's followers should be kept busy for a while. Yes, I think things will work out for Harlan after all. Come on, Spock, it's bedtime."

Chapter Nine

Harlan was staring bleary eyed into his coffee cup as the last of the others not already there arrived and straggled into The Lamp. Carrie was just starting her shift and was already delivering several coffees to the most recent arrivals. On seeing the rest come in she took one look at their collective appearance and headed straight back to the coffee pot for more.

"Tell them I'll be back in a minute with some brew for them, too. I need to put more coffee on. I can tell you're all in need of it."

"She's got that right," said Clifford, holding his head in his hands. "God, I don't often lose track of how many beer I've drank, but that was one of those nights. I'm going to have to ask Carrie if she knows, because I sure don't."

"All I know is it was good timing my next-door neighbour gave me some leftover pizza I could inhale to soak up some of the beer before I went to bed last night," said Harlan.

"Yeah, I was raiding the fridge last night too," said Nyota, rubbing her face as she sat down and grabbed the coffee in front of her as if it was a life preserver. "I never should have switched to drinking the white wine here. Got to talk to Carrie about it, because they can do a lot better with their wine choices for the price than that."

"I don't know how you people manage to talk and make sense before you've downed at least your first cup. Less talk, more coffee is my thinking," said Jordi, with a groan.

Gradually they all settled into their spots around the table, slowly sipping at their coffees and saying little. Harlan was torn between a desire to know what their thoughts were and his own need to drink more coffee. The thought of simply having Carrie bring an entire pot and leaving it on the table crossed his mind as Jordi called and motioned for more, holding his cup high so she would get the message. As she waved acknowledgement Jordi turned to the others to speak.

"God, I can feel that coffee moving through my brain like a tidal wave. Two more cups and I might feel human again. So while we are all working on that, I am curious. For the life of me I can't remember, because my memory from last night is still real fuzzy. Did we actually reach any conclusions about Arthur?"

"Don't think so," said Clifford, running his fingers through his rumpled hair and taking another gulp of coffee. "I was wondering that myself. All I remember is reaching a point where we collectively decided we were all too drunk to consider anything logically. Somehow we agreed to meet this morning, which amazes me we managed even that. Even more surprising, we all remembered to be here. So what do we all think? I figure this is all a conspiracy to keep us fat and happy so they can harvest us for food. You know, make the planet one big farm so they can feed us to their starving trillions of hungry aliens coming for us. Sorry, it's the cynic in me."

"God, didn't we sort this out last night?" said Keiko with a groan.

"No, actually, we didn't," said Spider. "We talked around it until we were all in danger of falling asleep under the table. But at some point I came to the conclusion I agree with Clifford. This is all way too innocuous. Someone is trying to lull us into a false sense of security. It's all just too weird to be true."

"At the risk of losing my sanity, I'm actually going to disagree," said Nyota, now toying with her second cup of coffee. "Well, the weird element is for certain, but I just don't have any sense of bad intent here. Arthur seems so mild mannered he could be someone's grandfather, for God's sake."

"Yeah, but is that enough reason to think they're actually friendly?" said Clifford.

"Well, why not? Besides, Arthur's been in this flying saucer for years and they haven't eaten us yet, have they?"

"True," said Spider, warming to the topic. "But then maybe the timeframes they are working with span decades. Who knows? But maybe she's right, maybe Arthur and his buddies really are nice aliens. Maybe they need help with bad aliens and are trying to protect us until we get our act together enough we can help them out? Or maybe there's a galaxy wide war going on and they are trying to find new recruits?"

Keiko rolled her eyes. "Good God, are you going to start rolling out the plot of every B movie you've ever seen?"

"Right," said Harlan. "Let's keep it under control, people. Look, there has to be some reason for this. If you buy what Arthur is saying, and I do, because there's been just too much weird shit happening to explain it all away, then there must be some kind of motive behind it all. I have to agree, I don't get a sense there is anything really bad behind this. But if I'm right, then what is God's name is going on? Any ideas?"

"A mass delusion? Collective insanity? Maybe someone poisoned us with a hallucinogenic drug that hasn't worn off yet?" said Keiko.

"Come on, Keiko," said Nyota. "Let's face it, something is going on here. I was as sceptical as you, but I am coming around to believing. Believing what is the question, mind you."

Keiko sighed. "Yes, you're right. I just don't like it when stuff makes no sense."

"Trying to steer clear of spending the rest of your life on a spaceship is also good motivation," said Jordi.

Keiko groaned, but before she could reply Nyota spoke to Deanna, who was still sitting and staring into her coffee cup.

"How about you, Deanna? You haven't said a word since you got here. What do you think? Or did you drink more of that white wine than I did last night?"

A corner of Deanna's mouth curled up ever so slightly, giving her a wry look, before she took yet another sip of her coffee and replied.

"Yeah, well, I was helping you with that wine last night, remember? I don't usually drink anywhere near that much. My head actually is a little fragile this morning. But what do I think? Hmm, I still don't know. Something isn't right."

Nyota frowned. "You said that before, more than once. What exactly are you referring to?"

Deanna shrugged. "Sorry, I still haven't put my finger on it. I know, that doesn't help much does it? But there is something about Arthur that just isn't right. He isn't like anyone or anything I've ever encountered before."

"What does that mean?"

"I really am having a hard time putting this into words, so bear with me. He doesn't feel right to me, but I don't understand why. I feel like I'm on the verge of sorting this out, but it's still eluding me. Drinking too much wine last night didn't help. Look, I'll give this more thought and I promise I'll focus more on it next time we see him. I'll figure this out one way or another. I do agree this is worth learning more about. Sorry, best I can offer."

"But do you at least think the aliens are friendly or what?"

This time Deanna frowned, pausing as she stared into her coffee cup before responding.

"Well...yes, I think so. I haven't sensed any spiritual danger since this started, if that is what you are asking me. I know most of you are sceptical about that kind of stuff, but I hope that gives you some reassurance. I am more attuned to that than any of you and you all know it. But this situation with Arthur, well, it's just...weird."

"You got that right," said Jordi. "You know, maybe Arthur is really an alien himself and that's why you can't sense him or whatever. Have you considered that possibility?"

"Actually, yes, but I've discounted the idea.

Don't know why, but that notion doesn't feel right. And I'm still not convinced we are in any danger."

"Okay, whatever you say. So what are we going to do about this? I'd like to plan my life a bit here. I do other stuff in my life besides chase weird aliens and government agents around."

"Well, we can sit around here for hours talking conspiracy theories, but I don't see how that gets us anywhere," said Nyota. "We need more time with Arthur. Every time I think about this I just have more questions. Hopefully we won't get interrupted again."

"I still don't get this," said Jordi. "I know Harlan says he disappeared, and I have to confess I don't understand how he was suddenly nowhere to be found yesterday, but I need some real proof. Yeah, he's got some weird government agents following him around, but I've got to be convinced. So Harlan, how do we get that and when?"

Harlan shrugged. "Arthur seems to show up on cue in the park when I arrive, so I suggest we just all meet there again and see what happens. Hey, I don't know. I suppose he might even appear here again, but if he hasn't showed up by now he likely won't, at least for today."

"How do we stop the government agents from showing up and interrupting things again?" said Nyota. "Do you think they are listening in to us making plans as we speak?"

"Arthur assured me he was jamming their ability to listen in to us, but I have a theory about how they keep finding us. I figure what they are doing is using our cell phones to locate us by GPS. Not hard to do if you have the right gear and you know who your targets are, I suppose. But the likelihood any of us are going to go anywhere or do anything without our electronic leashes is most unlikely. So I think we just trust Arthur to deal with it and see what happens. If they do show up, maybe we'll at least have gotten a bit more time with Arthur to ask questions before it gets crazy."

"Huh," said Spider. "Cell phones, I should have thought of that. Makes sense, though. It isn't a stretch to think they could pull that off. Probably not even breaking a sweat doing it, either."

"You know, I think Harlan may be right," said Keiko, pointing at the window beside their table looking out on the street. "I think Spider is right about not breaking a sweat, too. Correct me if I'm wrong, those are our friendly government spooks, are they not?"

Everyone turned as one to look where she was pointing to find a small black sedan cruising past. Two men wearing ball caps and sunglasses were inside. The windows were tinted, making it difficult to make out their features, but the tell-tale was one strange looking antenna attached to the roof of the car. As they all watched it was as if the occupants of the car sensed they were being observed and the car sped up, moving down the street to disappear within moments around the corner. As they all turned to look back at each other Spider began laughing.

"Damn, that has to have been them. Persistent bastards, aren't they? But I wonder what happened to their van? Maybe they are trying to throw us off their scent or something?"

"Huh," said Clifford. "Can't pack as much funky electronic shit into that little thing. Only one measly antenna, too. I mean, seriously. Any self-respecting government spook chasing aliens should have all the latest stuff to work with, don't you think? Doesn't make sense they'd switch."

"No, it doesn't," said Harlan with a frown, before shaking his head. 'Well, we aren't likely to find out why the change. Maybe Arthur will know?"

"You know, I'm beginning to think something nefarious is going on here," said Jordi.

"How so?" said Deanna, her face wearing a frown.

"Well, this guy Arthur just seems like some old loony to me. But these two? I don't know what you feel about them, but I have the distinct sense these guys aren't friendly. I think they are perpetrating something badass here and we could easily be their guinea pigs or their prey or whatever. Hell, maybe they are the aliens. I don't like it."

The frown stayed on Deanna's face. "I agree with you there is more to them than meets the eye, but I think you're stretching this more than a little, Jordi."

"Maybe, maybe not. I for one will be watching my back here."

"Good God, Jordi," said Keiko. "We already have two conspiracy theorists with Spider and Clifford around. We don't need more. But you know what you guys? I'll bet those two agents or aliens are just driving around the block. They wouldn't give up that easily."

"Hey, I think she could be right," said Spider. "You know, if we all get out on the sidewalk right now we could line up and say hi to them as they drive by the next time. Anyone with me?"

"I'm in," said Clifford. "Let's go."

"Me too," said Jordi.

As the three men got up in a rush and left, Keiko merely shook her head and turned back to the others.

"Lunatics. Right, what is the plan here? Do we even have one? I'm with Jordi on this, I have things to do this weekend."

Harlan shrugged once again. "Look, why don't we simply meet in the park tomorrow at noon? My money says Arthur will show up. Maybe we'll have company, maybe we won't. I can't predict what he is going to do, but let's see what happens."

As the others nodded agreement Keiko startled them all as she began laughing, pointing out the window again as she did. The others looked and began laughing aloud too. The black sedan appeared once again, turning the corner back onto the street outside, but this time it wasn't slowing down as it drove by. Clifford, Spider, and Jordi were all at the edge of the sidewalk, bent over and facing away from the car with their pants down to offer a full moon to the agents. Harlan looked to see the reaction and thought he could see just well enough into the car to make out frozen looks of disgust on the faces of the two men inside.

Chapter Ten

Harlan approached the clearing in the park the next day with trepidation, uncertain if Arthur really would join them or if all he would find was his two government shadows hiding somewhere nearby to watch. The others clustered around him obviously felt the same, for their heads were swivelling about in all directions like his to see what was waiting for them.

The day before they agreed to a suggestion from Jordi to meet near the park and go to where they all saw Arthur before in one group, the notion being several pairs of eyes would stand a better chance of ferreting out anyone watching or waiting for them. As added security, they all refrained from doing any messaging back and forth to each other about what their plans were.

As the clearing came into view Harlan smiled, for sitting at the park bench was Arthur. As Harlan walked up he took one last, long look around to confirm no one else was in the area. He waved at Arthur, who waved back.

"I was hoping you would be here, Arthur. Thanks for coming. My friends wanted to continue our conversation."

"I know," said Arthur, a smile on his face. "I was sure you'd figure out I would meet you here."

Harlan took a few moments to tell Arthur about the appearance of the agents the day before and the fact they were using a different vehicle as the others settled in around the two of them.

"So we are curious, Arthur? Did you have

something to do with those two using a different car?"

Arthur gave him a blank look and shook his head. "Nope, sorry. This is news to me."

"Huh, another mystery. And as far as you know, they aren't in the area today?"

Arthur paused for a moment as if looking inward, before looking back at Harlan.

"The ship says they aren't here at the moment. It will let me know if that changes."

"Excellent. The reason I ask is some of us are...hmm, more than a little suspicious of their motives. Anyway, we have more questions for you, if you don't mind?"

"No problem. What would you like to know?"

"Who wants to go first?" said Harlan, looking around the table. Clifford was the fastest to put his hand up.

"Right, I'd like to hear more details here. Take us back, if you can. How did you first meet your alien buddy? Or should I say, what happened when you were collected?"

"Sure. Collected is probably as good a word as any. The truth is I was actually collected twice. I know that seems weird. The first time I was out in the field late in the evening, just finishing up my day's work you understand, when I was surrounded by all these strange flashing lights. After that I have no memory until I woke up out in the loft of the barn. My wife was shaking me and asking if I was all right."

"That's it? You don't remember more?"

"No. We were both real puzzled, because it took

a while for me to come to my senses. She'd heard a commotion out in the barn and came to find me. I was late coming in for dinner too, so she knew something was up. When she came out to look around and discovered me, her first impression was that I was drunk. Of course, she quickly realized how ridiculous that notion was because my usual alcohol intake is one beer a week. Mind you, the fact all my clothes were on backwards might have had something to do with her questioning the possibility."

Arthur laughed, a distant look of reminiscence appearing on his face.

"Yes, we sat and puzzled over that for a long time, but there were no easy answers. I'm sure you can imagine how strange it all seemed. My wife and I are just simple farm people, you know? We knew of stories about people being taken and we wondered if that was what happened to me, but it all seemed so farfetched. As time went by with no explanation forthcoming, we decided to simply take a wait and see approach. We told no one, of course. Everyone would have thought I was a crazy person."

"Hmm. So you say that was the first time?" said Spider. "What happened the second time? Was it the same?"

"No, it was very different. We both got taken this time and we remember a lot more about what happened, although much of it is fuzzy too."

"Different in what way?"

"Well, I knew it was happening because of the weird lights around me again and for whatever reason this time I looked up. It was a big flying saucer, of course. Before I could do anything I was encircled in this cone of light. Next thing I know I'm lying on a table, basically so paralyzed I can't even lift a finger, but for whatever reason I was semi-conscious. This vague shape was moving around the table and I could sense it was doing things to me, but it wasn't clear what. I felt nothing, in case you are wondering. I could see out of the corner of my eye that my wife was there too, lying on another nearby table. The alien, because that's who I assume it was, went over and did things to her too, but I don't know what."

"Wow," said Nyota. "Was she in the field with you when you were collected?"

"No, all she remembers is she was outside working in her garden when a bunch of strange lights suddenly appeared all around her. Next thing she knew she was on the ship. Anyway, the really strange part was the telepathy. That took some getting used to."

"Telepathy?" said Harlan.

"Sure. How do you think I communicate with the ship? You see one of these fancy cell phones anywhere on me?"

"The alien must have implanted some kind of device in you to make that happen," said Clifford.

"Maybe," said Arthur, shrugging as he responded. "It doesn't really matter, does it? All I know is stuff appears in my mind that isn't any of my doing. Anyway, we were both shown around the ship and then sent back home. Thing is, we had a mission to accomplish before we could come back."

"A mission?"

"Well, by this time we knew the alien needed help and wanted us on the ship. We didn't feel threatened or anything, and the alien actually seemed nice about it all, so we decided to help. We like to help when anyone needs us, so while this maybe does seem strange, we didn't want to turn the alien away. So we went home, kind of put our affairs in order, and were brought back to the ship when we were done. We just sent a thought message we were ready and next thing we know we were on the ship for good. And we've been there ever since."

"What do you mean, put your affairs in order?"

"Well, we needed to dream up a story for everyone. Told them we were going to travel the world, maybe live and work elsewhere. We never had kids, so it was easy enough. We kept the farm to lease it out, but that was it."

"Huh," said Spider. "Well, this more or less jives with other people's stories about being collected. I know, I've researched this. First the victim is captured and is unable to resist being taken to the saucer. Then they get probed. The probing part is vague. People tend to make up sexual elements to it. Whether there actually was some sort of sex involved is debatable."

Arthur smiled. "If there was a sexual element to what was done to us, it's news to me and my wife. But I suppose there could have been. My wife and I have always enjoyed having fun with each other."

"Right, well, next is the telepathic part where there is some kind of communication with the alien and people usually see some of the spaceship. Then they get returned home, sometimes in a totally different location from where they were abducted. People report a sense of euphoria. Usually their clothes are maybe missing or have been torn or are rumpled or something. So everything Arthur is saying matches other stories. The one exception is being told to go home and transition from an old life to something completely different. Actually, it almost sounds like he was given a choice, too. That is very unusual. I've never heard that before."

"Hmm, I wonder," said Keiko. "Maybe all the other people being collected were deemed unsuitable, but Arthur and his wife fit the bill?"

"Could be," said Arthur. "Come to think of it I did notice a while back that the number of reports of abductions disappeared after we came on the scene."

"Okay, so all this history is nice, but I'm interested in right now," said Jordi. "I for one still need you to prove to me this isn't all just some mass hallucination. Can you probe somebody or something? Keiko and I will volunteer for the sex probes."

Keiko groaned while most of the others simply rolled their eyes.

"God, take a break, Jordi," said Nyota.

"Well, I think I did mention I don't do much in the way of probing anything other than farm animals. I just do my job and watch these days. But I do need a volunteer to replace me. I still think Harlan would make a fine choice, but if one of the rest of you is interested I suppose I can consider the notion. You really should have a partner with you, though. Anyone?"

"Well, that rules out virtually all of us," said Nyota. "Sorry to tell you this, Arthur. We're all a bunch of losers in the love department. None of us are romantically attached to anyone right now and the prospects for change don't look good."

"Harlan wants Keiko to join him, but I think she's being holding out for better," said Jordi. "I could be persuaded, though."

"Don't hold your breath waiting," said Keiko. "Yes, I think you are out of luck, Arthur.

Before he could respond Deanna, a silent participant to this point, surprised everyone by speaking up. The hint of frustration in her voice was obvious to all.

"God, this is just too strange. Arthur, I know not everyone believes this, but I am used to being able to feel people's energy. Everything alive has energy around it. But I simply can't figure out why you have no energy for me to sense and, frankly, it's pissing me off because I don't understand. My brain says you are as human as I am, but my other senses tell me otherwise. And what I am trying to do is figure out whether or not the alien or aliens really are friendly through connecting with you. So what is going on here? I need some help here."

Arthur smiled. "Yes, I can help. I'm actually sorry, I should have clarified this a while back I suppose. There is a reason you can't sense me. Here, let me show you. Touch my hand."

Deanna looked at his hand with one eyebrow raised, looked up at Arthur with the same question on her face for a moment, before she hesitantly reached out her own hand. A second later she jerked it back in utter surprise, for her hand passed right through Arthur and appeared on the other side. Shocked gasps of amazement, disbelief, and wonder came from all sides.

"Good God, I should have figured this out before now," said Spider, poking his own hand right through Arthur's arm. "You are a hologram."

"Yes, I expect that is what it's called," said Arthur. "The ship seems to prefer I appear like this unless my wife and I are actually going out for dinner some place. Not sure why. Anyway, whatever it is, the ship does a pretty good job, doesn't it? None of you realized there was anything strange, except for Deanna here."

"Of course, it all makes sense now," said Deanna, the look of relief on her face obvious. "God, I thought I was losing it for a while there. As a hologram you don't have anything like the same kind of energy around you that we all have. Well, this makes me feel better."

Deanna looked around the table at the others before continuing.

"See, I'm not crazy. None of you believed me, but I sensed it."

"Well, maybe the next time I'll come down in person and we can test whether you notice," said Arthur, a teasing look on his face. "But meanwhile, I'm going to leave you shortly. Your friendly government agents are making an appearance again. In fact, they have moments ago sent up yet another drone to try and check us out. It's on its way here. I give them credit, they are persistent."

Everyone looked up, but nothing was in sight yet, although the faint whine of small drone motor could be heard in the distance. Arthur smiled.

"So I'll take care of the drone this time. I suggest we meet here again tomorrow at lunch time. I expect your government friends may want to talk to you all sooner or later. Maybe sooner, because I expect they are getting frustrated at their lack of success. If they bother you too much, ask them to explain what goes on in Warehouse #27. They won't answer you, but it may give them pause."

"Warehouse #27?" said Clifford. "Okay, so what does go on in Warehouse #27?"

Arthur shrugged. "I have no idea. Really, I don't. But the ship just made that suggestion to me. If the ship wants me to know I expect it will tell me. The less we know might be better. I think the ship may have decided it's time to start protecting all of you. It may be getting annoyed with these persistent people, if a ship even has the capability to feel that way. Anyway, I'm off. See you tomorrow."

With a wave and one last look around the table, Arthur vanished from sight. In less than an eyeblink, he simply disappeared.

"Holy crap." said Jordi, his jaw hanging open.

"Damn," Keiko.

"Well, there you have it," said Harlan, watching the others now nervously looking around. "Any sceptics still left around here?"

A long silence descended among the group, before Spider finally broke it.

"Nope. Not anymore. Need time to wrap my

head around this."

And as he finished speaking a drone with what appeared to be camera and microphone equipment attached to it crashed hard to the ground twenty feet from where they were all sitting. Harlan laughed.

"He wasn't kidding when he said the ship would take care of it, was he?"

Chapter Eleven

They all sat staring in stunned silence at the mangled wreckage strewn about, waiting for whatever was coming next.

"Uh, Harlan?" said Deanna, finally breaking the spell everyone seemed to feel. "What do we do now? Should we all get up and scatter in different directions?"

"May be too late for that," said Keiko, pointing over their shoulders at the nearby street. "That white van that pulled up over there likely has our friendly agents in it. At least, I expect so, since it has a whole array of weird antennas on it like their black one did. I wonder why they have yet another new vehicle?"

"Yes, I'd say you're right," said Harlan. "Well, why don't we just stick around and see what happens? If we all run off it will look like we have something to hide or have done something wrong, which of course we have not. Besides, someone is getting out. Yes, they appear to be on their way to pay us a visit."

"Hmm, that's them all right," said Jordi.

Harlan saw the two agents were indeed present, now simultaneously exiting from the van. Both men slammed the doors of the van closed harder than necessary, making it clear to Harlan neither of the agents were pleased about what was happening.

As they drew closer Harlan became certain of it, as both men stalked stiffly toward the now destroyed drone. They paused by it only for the briefest moment, as the black agent named Ray reached down to turn the device over, obviously looking to see how badly damaged it was. He dropped it to the ground and turned to glare at his partner with a look of disgust on his face. Harlan sensed that beneath the surface Ray was steaming with anger. The two men turned as one to face Harlan and his friends, walking over in unison to come closer to speak to them.

"Right," said the agent named Larry. "Any of you know what happened with this or have anything to do with it?"

Everyone remained silent, so to fill the void Harlan spoke up.

"I assure you, gentlemen, we had nothing to do with damaging your drone."

"Of course not. It was the old man, wasn't it? You all know who we are talking about. We could see he was here with you from the distance as we drove up. So how did he do it, huh? And where did he go?"

"Maybe he used a magic wand? And as far as we know he just disappeared into thin air. We don't know for sure where he went," said Spider.

Ray turned and glared at Spider, but said nothing, his look daring Spider to continue. Clifford thrust his head forward, a pugnacious look on his face as he spoke up instead.

"Are you accusing us of something? If you are, why don't you call the cops? Let's see what they think of this. Maybe they'll start asking questions you don't want to answer, like why a couple of mysterious government agents are spying on honest citizens?"

"So, Harlan?" said Larry, ignoring Clifford completely. "Have you thought about our offer? We really could use your help. And we could make it worth everyone's while to do so. What do you say?"

"Hmm, still thinking about it, Larry. I needed to have a talk with my friends here about it. To be honest, we are questioning your motives somewhat."

"Look, we are only trying to do the best we can for our country. Like all patriotic citizens should."

"Oh, please," said Spider, rolling his eyes. "We all love our country. But we're all citizens of this planet, too. We just need some convincing you guys actually have the best interests of the world in mind. You know, find some alien technology, share it with everyone so we can feed starving millions, make life easier for all of humanity, that kind of stuff."

"Tell me," said Ray. "Does the world you live in have rainbow-coloured unicorns in it, too? It must, because I don't think you're in the same world as everyone else. There are plenty of other governments out there that wouldn't hesitate to use...hmm, some new technology to do very bad things to us. Surely you understand that?"

"I think we do, gentlemen. The problem is we don't really know any more than you do what we are dealing with here," said Harlan. "I personally would be concerned if something innocent ended up being used for dark purposes. By anyone, not just you. You follow?"

Larry rolled his eyes. "Look, let's see if I have this straight. You don't know what you are dealing with, but you don't trust us either, because you don't trust your own government to do the 'right' thing, whatever that may be. Correct?"

"Yeah, that's probably about right. At least, for now."

"Okay, I will try one more time to help you understand. We do not intend anything nefarious. We have to investigate what is going on here. We don't know if this old man actually means us harm. And yes, if we find something important and new, of course the government will want to explore it. I assure you, our superiors have the best of intentions. But you also need to understand they will not be swayed from doing the job we need to do. We don't understand what is going on here and, until that changes, we will not let anyone or anything stand in our way. If my superiors lose patience our approach may change, and it might not be for the better."

"What exactly does that mean?" said Jordi, with an edge to his voice. "That sounds like a threat."

"You can take it however you want. Look, we have no interest in making your lives more difficult. We would rather do the opposite. As I said, we would prefer to make cooperation with us worth your while."

"No, tell us more," said Clifford. "How exactly could you make things worse? You're already following us around and putting pressure on us with no justification."

"No justification?" said Ray, a scowl creasing his face and his voice rising. "What do you call slashing all of our tires so badly they were all completely flat? What do you call cat pee on practically everything both inside and outside our van?"

"Ray, you need to calm..." said Larry, rolling his eyes again, but Ray interrupted him, this time letting the full extent of his anger show all the way through.

"And while we are at it, I want to know which one of you dumped the cat shit on the driver's seat of the van! I'll be you all thought it was pretty funny, huh?"

The two agents stood there glaring at the stunned, blank looks on everyone's faces as the people digested what he had said. Deanna was the one who finally processed the implications of it and spoke up, looking directly at Ray.

"Oooh, I get it. I'll bet one of you sat on the cat shit. It was you, wasn't it? I guess it would be kind of squishy to sit on. Have to get your clothes dry cleaned, did you?"

The rest of them burst into laughter as they too finally understood what happened to make the agent so angry. Ray clenched his fists in frustration and glared at Deanna, but Larry reached over to put a hand on his shoulder.

"Ray, let me deal with this. Right, so what do you know about this?"

Harlan was the first among them to master himself, because while he too thought it amusing another part of his mind was trying to process what was going on. That Arthur had made no mention of anything like this was puzzling.

"Well, this explains it," said Spider. "We were wondering why you suddenly appeared driving a car and now a different van. You missed all your high-tech toys having only a car, huh?"

"Forgive me if I don't believe you had nothing to do with this, asshole," said Ray, still scowling.

"Ray..." said Larry, a warning tone to his voice.

"Gentlemen, "said Harlan, trying to add a soothing tone to his voice. "I can assure you none of us were involved with whatever happened to your van. And we have no idea who might have done it."

"Uh huh, so you say. Well, let's turn this around. Perhaps you could try understanding our point of view. Someone did something to us, and to our minds you all fall into the suspect category. I really wouldn't advise continuing that kind of behaviour if one of you are the culprit. We could make your lives a lot more difficult than they are right now, you know."

"You keep saying that, but it sounds like an empty threat to me," said Jordi.

"Oh really? We know more about all of you than you realize."

"Yeah? Like what, exactly?"

"Well, for starters, I won't say who, but one of you is likely bisexual and isn't ready to admit it," said Larry, folding his arms and plastering a knowing look on his face. "We wouldn't want to go exposing someone or the details of how exactly we know that, now would we?"

As one Harlan and his friends all turned to look at Keiko. She wore a look like a startled rabbit for a brief second before she rolled her eyes and looked around at the rest of them.

"Oh right, you all point the finger at me," she said, an outraged tone to her voice. "That could be any of you and you all know it."

"Yeah, maybe or maybe not," said Larry. "And then there is one of you that has some rather questionable financial dealings going on right now. May cause a few issues if any of that comes to light sooner than later. Some people, like the tax man, might not be too happy about it. Maybe some borderline fraud, too."

This time everyone turned as one to look at Jordi, who reacted exactly the same as Keiko.

"What? What have I done?" said Jordi, a tone of indignation rising in his voice, too.

"Oh, I think you know very well what I am talking about."

"Maybe your get rich quick scheme might have a few holes in it, asshole," said Ray. "Just saying."

"Come on Jordi," said Spider. "The jig is maybe up with whatever it is you're up to. There isn't anyone else around here that fits this description."

"Larry?" said Ray. "Let's not forget they were all smoking that funny stuff back when it wasn't legal anywhere. Who knows what all they got up to? I'll bet if we dug into that we could find all kinds of good stuff. We could pass that on to their employers. That could maybe cause some grief."

"Oh, for God's sake, and you two are pure as the driven snow?' said Nyota. "Give me a break. No one is perfect. If you fired everyone who has ever smoked pot you'd suddenly find at least a third of your workforce was gone."

"You know what I think?" said Clifford. "I figure you two are rookies. They sent you two out to do the dirty work, make cheap threats and intimidate us. Maybe you're in training or something. When do you get to take the training wheels off, huh? Or maybe you just drew the short straw for this assignment."

Larry groaned and shook his head, while Ray scowled in Clifford's direction and responded.

"Listen, asshole, think what you want. My colleague here explained the situation to you. Think about it, all of you, and let us know before our patience runs out."

"Yes," said Larry, this time scowling himself as he looked at Spider. "And put the damn phone away. I can see you trying to record us."

"Why wouldn't I?" said Spider. "It's not every day I get a video of real spooks from Area 51. Hey, we almost forgot. We need to ask you about what goes on in warehouse number 27. Anything you can share with us?"

The change in their demeanour was instantaneous as frozen looks appeared on the faces of both agents. They slowly looked at each other from the corner of their eyes before turning back to glare at Spider.

"What makes you ask that?" said Larry, with an angry edge to his voice.

"Just curious. Some rumour going around on the net or something like that. So what gives?"

"There is nothing going around on the net about that," barked Larry, as he allowed his frustration to come through in his voice. "Tell...us...what you know."

"Are you deaf? I'm the one that asked the question. If I knew what was going on in this warehouse, why would I be asking you about it?"

"You know, I've about had all I can take of your attitude..." said Ray, before Larry cut him off.

"Forget it, Ray. He is just trying to antagonize us and they aren't going to cooperate. And we both know how they knew to ask about it. We need to discuss this with the others. Come on, let's get out of here."

'You know, I'm curious about you two," said Spider. "Are those your real names or is it actually too much of a coincidence you have those names, Larry and Ray?"

Both men gave each other a puzzled side glance, obviously hoping the other knew what Spider was referring to.

"Oh, come on," said Spider, his eyebrows raised in doubt. "A couple of Area 51 agents that don't read science fiction? You know, stuff about Martians or things like ringworlds? It's beyond coincidence."

The two agents stared at Spider with disbelief of their own before turning to leave as one. Larry paused and looked over his shoulder at Harlan.

"I have no idea what he is talking about. But Harlan? It's not too late to cooperate. Think about it."

Both men stooped to gather up the debris of their drone briefly before stalking away. As they did Jordi spoke up, loud enough everyone was certain the agents could hear him.

"Hey, I know. I'll bet these guys are really the bad guys in disguise. Russians, I'll bet. These two are such amateurs they have to be. We should just report them to the cops."

"There may not be anything on the net about area 51 and warehouse 27 yet, but there sure will be now," called out Spider, grinning broadly as he did. "We've even got videos to post. Man, you simply can't make this stuff up, can you?"

Harlan thought for a moment the two agents were going to stop and come back, but neither did, although he was certain they both heard what was being said. He shook his head.

"You two are going to get us into trouble yet."

Spider shrugged. "So what? Maybe if we start some shit going around online they'll back off and stop bothering us."

"I think we should just send some messages around about maybe going to the media," said Keiko. "These two really are becoming a pain, but maybe the threat of a spotlight will make them back off a bit. And if they really are monitoring some of our communications we'll have to refrain from putting anything about future meetings with Arthur in messages."

"I agree," said Deanna. "So let's all make a point of not referencing we will be back here tomorrow at lunch in any communication. Well, the show is over so I'm off."

The others all nodded and got up to go their separate ways. As they were going the same direction, Harlan fell in step beside Keiko. They were both silent for a moment, before they turned to each other to speak at the same time. Both of them laughed and Keiko finally spoke, a rueful look on her face.

"You go first."

Harlan shrugged as they continued walking. "Well, I was just going to ask if you still think I'm a total flake, or if you are beginning to see some potential in me?"

Keiko was silent for a moment before responding. "You do have your flake moments, but I can't deny any of what I saw. Still don't understand this, but I guess none of us do. And I have to admit...well, give me a little more time, okay?"

"Okay."

A silence descended once again, before Harlan finally broke it.

"Well, that was all I wanted to know. You were going to say something?"

"I...I was wondering what you thought about when they brought up the sexuality thing."

Harlan shrugged and gave her a small laugh.

"I know everyone looked at you, but I'd say there are other possible suspects that could fit the description. And for the record, I couldn't care less who it is. If it is you and you decide not to share that, it's your business. It doesn't change how I feel about you, if that is what you are wondering. I believe in you."

Keiko stopped and turned to look up at Harlan for a moment, before reaching up to kiss him on the cheek.

"Thank you for that. I'll see you tomorrow."

Harlan was silent as she walked away toward her home, knowing she needed to be alone.

***

That evening Harlan was sitting on his deck with

a beer, still puzzling over the events of the day, when the familiar voice of his neighbour broke his reverie.

"You look deep in thought," said Isaac. "I've been standing here for almost a minute and you never noticed. Can I join you for a drink?"

"Uh, sure. Come on over."

As Harlan spoke he looked down to see Spock was already purring and winding himself around his leg.

"Spock has already invited himself anyway," added Harlan, reaching down to scratch behind the cat's ear.

Isaac settled into the other chair, putting his own drink on the table, before turning to Harlan. Spock jumped into Isaac's lap the second he was seated.

"So why so deep in thought? Let me guess, more developments with your space farmer, is it?"

"Hmm, yes. And with our government agents, too. It was all a little surreal today."

Harlan took a deep pull of his beer before relaying everything that happened since his last conversation with Isaac. When he finally finished, Isaac simply nodded.

"This gets more interesting all the time. Warehouse number 27, huh?" he said, rubbing his chin in thought. "Haven't heard that one before."

"Neither had we, until Arthur mentioned it. Those two agents looked like we'd caught them eating doughnuts when they were supposed to be on a diet. I think some of the others are going to start posting stuff online about it just to annoy them. Who knows, maybe they'll back off a bit. But the weird part I don't get is what happened to their van. Arthur never said anything about whether it was his doing and I kind of think he would have told us if it was. That is what I was puzzling over when you showed up."

"Hmm, well, strange things do happen now and again. Who knows, maybe it was Spock being a bad kitty?" said Isaac with a laugh, scratching behind the cat's ear. "How about it, Spock? Have you been naughty again?"

Harlan could only smile. "I guess he could be a suspect for the cat pee and poop they claim was everywhere, but I just can't figure out who would have put it all over the place in their van. And then there is how someone would have managed to slash all of their tires so badly they all went flat. Weird."

"Spock does have sharp claws, you know," said Isaac, an odd smile creasing his face as he spoke.

Harlan laughed this time, certain Isaac was being flippant. But the puzzle of who could have done the deed and gotten away with it remained in the back of his mind the rest of the evening.

And Spock simply sat in his owner's lap, wearing the same curious expression Harlan was becoming all too familiar with and was certain could only be the cat version of a grin.

Chapter Twelve

Everyone showed up in the park earlier than the agreed upon time. Harlan was the last to arrive, having actually gone into the office to do some work before telling his co-workers he would be gone the rest of the day. Neither Keiko nor Jordi appeared at work. As he walked up to where they were all sitting he peered about only to realize Arthur was nowhere in sight. The Area 51 agents were also absent from the scene. Harlan looked at Keiko and Jordi as he spoke.

"What happened to you two today?"

Both of them wore sheepish looks on their faces. Keiko finally grimaced and confessed.

"Couldn't sleep last night. Called in sick because my mind kept going over and over everything that happened yesterday."

"Same for me," said Jordi with a shrug. "But we're not alone. Everyone else here did the same thing."

"Seriously?" said Harlan. "I'm the only one of all of us that went to work?"

"Give us a break, Harlan," said Nyota. "You've been dealing with this a bit longer than we have. I confess I wasn't really taking any of this seriously until yesterday. Everyone else here is pretty much in the same boat."

"The good news is we have a plan now, Harlan," said Clifford.

"We do? For what?"

"For dealing with our government friends if they come to annoy us again. A little payback."

"Tell me."

When Clifford finished Harlan smiled in response. "I see. And we are ready to implement this, I take it?"

As Clifford nodded, Harlan's smile broadened. "Well, that has a chance to succeed, I'd say. They aren't here yet, but they have been persistent. Who dreamt this up?"

This time both Spider and Clifford looked at each other and grinned in response.

"Of course, I didn't really need to ask, did I?"

They were all so focused on Harlan none of them realized Arthur was now present until his voice cut into the conversation.

"Hello everyone. My, you're all a bit early, aren't you?"

The sheepish looks reappeared on a few of the faces as Harlan spoke.

"I think they are all anxious to learn more about you, Arthur."

From the corner of his eye Harlan saw the one exception was Deanna, who was frowning.

"Arthur?" she said. "You're a hologram again, aren't you? I thought you were maybe coming in person this time."

Arthur smiled. "You really are very perceptive. Yes, I am a hologram again. I proposed coming in person to the ship, but it didn't want me doing that. I don't know why. Probably something to do with these government people, I suppose. Anyway, it's not a problem for any of you, I expect."

"So Arthur," said Spider. "Now that we've been digesting all this a bit I think we all have more questions for you. I for one would like to know for sure what you know about other aliens out there. That is, are there any others? If so, are they nice? Have there ever been alien wars with each other? What sort of weapons do they use if there are wars between them?"

Arthur laughed. "Okay, slow down a bit. Lots of questions. First of all, I don't know for sure if there are others out there or not. I've never seen anything to confirm it either way. And yes, I have posed the question to the ship, but haven't gotten any answers. It seems to want me to just focus on the job at hand and not get distracted by other stuff, as strange as that may sound. So I can't say for sure about other aliens, let alone whether there have been alien wars. I can tell you my alien ship does have weapons. I actually have one. It's kind of a...well, I suppose you'd call it a blaster or something."

Expressions of surprise appeared on everyone's faces in the stunned silence that followed. Spider's jaw dropped open as his eyes went wide, before he mastered himself and spoke up.

"Oh, my God, Arthur. I would really, really enjoy seeing it. Can you show us?"

Arthur shrugged. "I guess. Don't know why not? Give me a minute, I'll be right back."

As he finished speaking he vanished out of sight.

"Good Lord, it's going to take me a while to get used to seeing that," said Keiko. "My brain simply doesn't want to accept what I just saw."

Before anyone else could speak Arthur blinked back into sight in the same spot he was moments before. This time, however, he held up an object for everyone's inspection. A stunned silence followed as everyone took time to process what they were seeing.

"Uh, Arthur?" said Harlan. "Am I missing something? That looks like a banana."

"Yes, it does, doesn't it? But I assure you, it is far more than that."

"Okay," said Spider. "I'll believe you. But what does it do? How does it work? Specifically, which is the business end of it? Have you ever used it?"

Arthur laughed. "So many questions. Like everything else on this ship, it seems to work by connecting with my thoughts. Here, let me show you."

Grasping one end of his blaster, Arthur pointed the banana at Spider and pushed on a specific spot with his forefinger. Spider automatically recoiled backwards in anticipation of being fried. To everyone's shock, a small, pulsing, but tightly focused orange coloured energy beam appeared from the opposite end, extending a foot outwards from it.

"Don't worry, I won't hurt you with it. As you can see, the beam isn't going very far. That's because I told it to do that. If you were a threat I obviously would have put no such limitation on it."

"Uh, so what would happen if it did hit me? Cook me on the spot or blow a hole through me?"

"Darned if I know," said Arthur with a shrug and an apologetic smile. "I've never actually used it on anybody. All I know is it will incapacitate someone. The ship has made me take it along for self-defence whenever I actually do come down in person."

Nyota grinned. "So you have to explain to all the women you meet that it really is a banana in your pocket and you're not just glad to meet them, huh?"

Arthur looked puzzled for a moment and then laughed.

"A banana in my pocket? What...oh, yes, young lady, I think I have heard that line somewhere before, but I've never needed to explain myself, though. I'm too old to be of interest."

As he finished speaking he looked down at the blaster, pushing on a different spot with his finger this time. The beam winked out, leaving the blaster looking exactly like a simple banana once more. Unaware of the irony, Arthur stuck it in his pocket, which elicited a few titters of laughter from the women around the table.

Jordi rolled his eyes and spoke up. "Arthur? Can you bring us up to the ship for a tour? Maybe go out for a little cruise with it? I'd love to see how fast it can go. If it can fly circles around our jet fighters, it's going to have a major power source and propulsion system. But really, the reason I ask is I think most of us are all seriously considering volunteering if Harlan doesn't want the replacement job. It would be nice to have a better idea of what we are getting into, though. I'd like to see how you control the ship, get it to go places, right?"

"Hmm. Well, I think I mentioned it's all done with thoughts. If the ship doesn't want to do something, I find out soon enough. As for coming for a visit, I'll have to pose that idea to the ship and see what happens. Not sure it would work, because I'm supposed to be focusing on only one person along with maybe a spouse to come with them."

Arthur paused a moment in obvious thought before continuing.

"Hmm, I guess there would be enough room for everyone. It's kind of strange, I don't think the ship is really all that big, although I always seem able to find some nook I can be on my own. Just when I think I know my way around in it, there are days I come across a place I've not seen before. Anyway, there is only one way to find out if the ship will let me bring you all up, I suppose. I'll try if you all want me to."

"Oh, I think we'd all love a tour of the ship, even if we aren't chosen," said Deanna. "But forget about these cowboys and their fascination with your toys, I'm interested in knowing what you really think about all this? You've got to have some theories or ideas?"

Arthur shrugged. "Yes, my wife and I have worked our way through a bunch of possibilities over the years. We usually end up discarding them, because there are just too many unknown elements here. The one we held onto for a long time was the idea that it's descendants of our own ancestors keeping an eye on us."

"Come again? How would that work?"

"Well, it boils down to motivation. Look, humans have been around a long time. Suppose we were an advanced civilization, enough that we took to space and colonized other worlds. Meanwhile, back here on earth we weren't as advanced as we thought we were and we managed to blow ourselves back to the stone age. You have to admit, humans are a rather aggressive species. But over the centuries we work our way back to where we are now. In the meantime, our ancestors maybe had their own problems, but they are now even more advanced and have come in search of us. They find us and are still figuring out what to do now they are back. Give us all this fancy technology and welcome us into the fold, only to have us blow ourselves to pieces again?"

Arthur paused and looked around the table. "Yes, I know. It's a stretch. My wife and I acknowledge there could be plenty of other explanations. Bottom line, we don't know what is motivating our alien or aliens to have me keeping watch. What we do know for sure is it is somehow very important that we don't let humanity blow itself up. There has to be a reason."

"So, like, help me understand," said Spider, rubbing his face in puzzlement. "Tell us again, how exactly would you stop that from happening?"

"It's strange, I know. Basically, it all boils down to my job, which is I am to monitor things here. If I sense it is going badly downhill, I am to alert the ship. I think the ship has some kind of technology that would disable all of our machines and fighter planes and everything from working. I have no idea how it works. Who knows? What I have come to understand is space is really, really big and there are things out there we know nothing of, let alone comprehend. The ship took us out beyond our solar system once when we asked for a little trip, you see. We know how big the universe truly is."

"So the ship has some sort of a magic, freeze

everything ray or something like that?"

"I guess."

"And what would happen after that?"

"Good question. Maybe the alien would return. I have no explanation for it."

"This is making my brain hurt again," said Keiko.

"Ditto," said Clifford. "But what about..."

"Sorry to interrupt," said Arthur, his head jerking up. "The ship has just told me we are going to be visited again. Have to give them credit, those fellows are persistent. And that means I will have to vanish on you once more."

"Arthur," said Spider. "Before you go? Can I suggest meet us at The Lamp in a couple of hours, please? We have a little plan at the ready to hopefully get rid of them, at least for a little while. We 've all taken the day off and we'd really like to continue this conversation."

Arthur laughed. "You do? Your turn to make their life difficult, is it? All right, I'll be there. I'll be back as a hologram again. While I'm waiting I'll see if the ship will consider bringing you all up for a tour. See you soon."

Arthur disappeared from sight again. Nyota closed her eyes and shook her head roughly, as if trying to free it of something unwanted clinging to her.

"God, that's weird. My mind doesn't want to accept that."

"Well, Arthur was right yet again," said Harlan, pointing off to the street. The agents were nearby once again and were even back to riding in their usual black van with antennas all over it as well.

"Right. Everyone know what to do?" said Spider. As everyone nodded, he smiled.

"Okay, I'm on it. See you soon."

Chapter Thirteen

Harlan watched with his remaining friends as Spider rose from his seat and headed off in a different direction, away from the one the government agents would appear if they came over to try talking to them again. The black van slowed as it drove past, then made its way further down the street. It finally pulled into an empty parking spot almost out of sight from where Harlan was sitting and parked.

"So what do we do now?" asked Harlan, looking over at Clifford.

"We annoy them. We all sit here for a while and look like we are conspiring to do something sneaky, which we are. We know they can't pick up on anything we are saying because you are here, so it doesn't matter what we say. I figure we wait until we're certain they've deployed the drone again before we make our move. They'll have to either abandon it or do something desperate to park it out of sight in a hurry and hope no one finds it. Either way, I'm sure it will piss them off."

Almost ten minutes later there were no signs of the agents, but Clifford suddenly pointed at a cluster of nearby trees.

"Here we go, look just above the top of that tall tree. They must have snuck out of the van. Time to go, everyone."

They all looked where Clifford was pointing and saw right away he was correct, as the agent's drone was in the air once again. Hovering slightly above the treetops in an obvious attempt to remain unobserved was a drone similar in size and shape to the other one the agents used before. As one Harlan and his friends got up from the tables they were sitting at and made their way towards the street.

"Let's pick up the pace everyone," urged Clifford. "Look over your shoulders to see if they are following us. It'll make us look guilty as hell."

Clifford led them to the nondescript white van he rented earlier that day and parked nearby on the street. The van was big, with an extra-large extended passenger compartment on it, making it large enough to hold everyone comfortably. Once he was certain they were all in, Clifford jumped into the driver's seat and started the engine. As he pulled out of the parking spot he grinned.

"So far so good. I think we've caught them by surprise. Ah, yes, we have indeed. Smile and wave at the government agents, everyone!"

They all obliged as Clifford steered them past the black van still parked in its spot. The agent named Larry was sitting in the driver's seat with a startled look on his face, while Ray was bursting out of the nearby bushes with a drone in his hands. He stumbled on something in his rush to get back and flailed about to no avail, landing face first on the grass. As he did the drone slipped from his grasp and smashed to the ground on the concrete sidewalk, breaking into several pieces.

"Wow, the way these guys go through drones I hope they have an understanding boss with a big budget," said Nyota, laughing as she turned back to watch what was happening.

"They're the government. Our tax dollars will

pay for more," said Clifford. "Hey, someone put some tunes on. Might as well enjoy our little scenic drive here. I have to pay attention and make sure we don't lose our friends. Yes, let's dawdle a bit. Ah, here's a nice red light I can stop for a while at. They can catch up."

"Don't you think they'll be suspicious?" asked Deanna.

"Maybe," said Clifford, shrugging as he glanced in the rear-view mirror. "But they don't have much choice, do they? Harlan is their target that will lead them to Arthur. And as I hoped, they have pulled out all the stops to follow us. We're in business, people. Okay, Harlan, you can make the call."

Pulling out his cell Harlan tapped the number set up long ago in his contacts. After a brief conversation, he ended the call and looked at Clifford.

"Thirty minutes. They are busy right now."

"No problem," said Clifford. "Let's go on a drive downtown. It'll be that much harder for them to follow us."

Thirty minutes later they pulled up briefly on the street to let Harlan get out. As the van pulled away and Harlan ducked into the doorway of his destination as fast as he could, he could see out of the corner of his eye their pursuers pause much further down the street. He smiled to himself, certain the manoeuvre was accomplished so fast the two agents would be struggling with uncertainty over who got out and what they should do next.

Five minutes later he walked out the door of the restaurant with two large pizzas and a plentiful supply of napkins in hand. Clifford and the others were all grinning broadly as they waited for him, having simply driven around the block a couple of times.

The black van with one of the agents was only now rounding the corner back onto the street following them in hot pursuit. Deanna pointed to a doorway across the street and down a short distance where the other agent was trying unsuccessfully to hide himself. Harlan waved at the man and got back into the van.

"What now, Clifford? Are we going to drive around some more or have we annoyed them sufficiently?" said Harlan.

"I expect we've achieved our goal, so it's back to the park. Besides, we can't let the pizza get cold, now can we?"

When they returned to the park this time Clifford managed to get the van back into exactly the same spot he used earlier. The black van cruised slowly past and everyone made a point of waving to the agents. Within minutes of sitting back down and digging into the pizzas the sign they knew the plan was working came.

"Looks like you and Spider have them figured out, Clifford," said Harlan. "Here they come."

"Of course. We've pissed them off and now they have to come and chew us out for it. We knew they wouldn't be able to resist."

As the two agents stalked closer it wasn't difficult for Harlan to see past the frozen looks on their faces and sense the simmering frustration boiling inside. They stopped near the table and stood silently, arms folded, as if waiting for a response.

"Hi, guys," said Clifford, adding an exaggerated, cheery note to his voice and look to his face. "Nice to see you again so soon. Didn't realize you were going to show up, otherwise we'd have ordered some pizza for you, too."

Larry the agent glared at him for a moment, before looking around the table and scowling.

"Very funny. Or at least I expect you all think it's funny. But it's not. You lead us on a wild goose chase, while we are trying to make sense of something that may affect our national security. Have none of you any sense of responsibility?"

"We were hungry," said Keiko. "What, are you expecting us to check in with you in advance for anything we do? Go to the bathroom, maybe?"

"Stow it, for God's sake," said Ray. "We aren't interested in your bathroom habits, okay? Look, what did the old man do or say today? Is he coming back? We'd just like to talk to him, that's all. Could you at least pass that message on to him? We mean him no harm, we only want to learn more."

"Don't you think he knows that, gentlemen?" said Nyota. "I mean, really, he'd likely have figured that out by now. Maybe he simply doesn't trust you."

"And why would he not trust us?"

"Do I really have to answer that?"

"Look, we get it," said Larry. "Please do us a favour. One little favour. It's all we ask. Just tell him we would like to talk to him, no strings attached. We promise not to abduct him or do bad stuff."

As he finished speaking Clifford's phone pinged to signal an incoming text message, which Clifford promptly checked. Clifford smiled as he finished and looked around.

"The wheels are in motion."

"Wheels? What wheels?" said Ray, a suspicious tone to his voice.

"Yes, gentlemen, I promise we will deliver your message," said Harlan. "I can't guarantee what the reception will be or whether he'll agree to what you want, but I will do as you ask. Happy now?"

Larry peered hard at him with a wary look on his face, as if trying to confirm Harlan wasn't pulling his leg, but he obviously decided Harlan was telling the truth.

"Um...yes. Yes, I am happy. I appreciate your cooperation, Harlan. I..."

"Hey," said Ray, interrupting his partner mid-sentence. "Something is going on here. Where is the other guy? Larry, one of them is missing."

Larry scanned their faces and then their immediate surroundings in response, before he finally let his gaze return to Harlan.

"Ray is right. What is happening here?"

"What is happening is we've enjoyed our lunch and now we're all going to go our separate ways," said Clifford. "Come on everyone, finish your pizza and let's go."

Everyone wolfed down their remaining food and rose to leave, all under the suspicious gaze of the two agents. As they all split up Harlan took pity on the two agents, lingering behind long enough to speak to them once more.

"A word with you, gentlemen? In my experience, approaching people in a positive way will get you a lot further towards what you want than the opposite tactic. Just saying. And I really will pass on your request to the old man. Can't say I'm optimistic he'll do what you want, but who knows? Good day, sirs."

***

Spider pointed down the street to where the black van was parked as he spoke to the two police officers in the marked patrol car.

"Thanks for attending, officers. I know this sounds weird, but I simply couldn't let this pass. As you can see this is a really strange looking van. I have no idea what all those odd antennas are for on that thing, but they certainly caught my eye. As I told them on the emergency line, the other fellow I ran into who overheard them talking had to leave. He told me the two guys were talking about aliens and trying to find the nearest military base. God knows why. I know, this is sounding totally crazy. I wouldn't have paid him any mind, but for the fact this van looks so completely unusual. And then after he left I looked closer and saw the van has no rear licence plate. The two guys inside got out and wandered off into the park over there a little while ago, so I decided to play it safe and call this in."

The officer in the driver's seat frowned and turned to look at his partner, who pointed down the street to the van.

"You know, I think he's right, at least about one thing. It's a ways away, but I can't see a plate on that thing."

"And hey, there they are, coming back," said Spider, pointing over at the park.

The two agents were indeed returning to their van, but they were also both staring hard at Spider and the police car as they went.

"Is it my imagination, officer, or did those two pick up the pace back to their van when they saw us just now?" said Spider.

Reaching the van, the two agents jumped in as one. Seconds later the van's engine roared to life and it pulled out of its parking spot to speed away.

"I don't think that was your imagination," said the officer in the driver's seat, shifting the police car out of park. "Thank you for calling that in. We will take this from here."

The police car's emergency lights came on, followed by the wail of its siren as it sped off to chase after the now distant van. Spider watched them drive off, before turning to leave. Moments later came what sounded like a small fender bender car accident. Spider looked back to see the black van had inadvertently struck the rear end of another vehicle in their apparent haste to get away. The police car was pulling up behind them even as the two agents got out to look at the damage.

Spider laughed as he glanced briefly at the large, thick bush by the side of the street where the van's licence plate was still hidden. After making certain one last time that no one was likely to find it, he smiled and walked away.

***

Harlan and the others met up at the prearranged spot two blocks away on the other side of the park.

Spider was the last to arrive and he reassured them the plan was working as they made their way to The Lamp. Arthur was already there, sitting at their usual table when they arrived. They waited until after everyone ordered drinks and Carrie dropped them off before telling Arthur of their latest encounter with the agents. Arthur laughed.

"Most amusing. A little harmless fun with them, I guess."

"Well, I'm sure they probably won't view it as such," said Harlan. "But we aren't beholden to them. I did, however, promise to pass on a message from them."

Arthur laughed again once Harlan finished telling him of the agent's request.

"No, I don't think I'll be agreeing to that. Even if I wanted to, I think the ship would object. The less they know, the better. But speaking of the ship, I promised to check on whether it would consider letting all of you come up for a tour of it."

"Oh, yes," said Spider. "Please tell us it said yes."

"Well, not really, but it didn't say no either. See, the thing is I think it is confused, if that's even possible for what is likely some sort of machine to be in that state. My job is to find a replacement for my wife and me, you understand. Bringing a whole bunch of people up to see the ship doesn't seem to fit what it is expecting. I guess it just doesn't understand why a tour of the ship is important, or even why you view the ship as unusual. I know that probably sounds strange, but, well, this is an alien ship, right?"

"So, you're saying it needs a rationale to do that," said Nyota. "Maybe you could tell it you are interviewing candidates and have several possibilities? We don't all need to come at the same time."

"Hmm," said Arthur, frowning a little. "Well, the ship has a thing about secrecy, too. Hard to make all this work, I guess. But really, I think the problem here is you all want to see the ship. Can you help me understand, please? What is your motivation? And I don't mean collectively, I mean each of you individually. I know this may seem strange, but I am very serious about what is needed here. As crazy as all this may seem, I've got a job to do and I take it seriously. If you are just interested in seeing the ship for the thrill of it, then I am dealing with the wrong person. Or people. Am I making sense about this?"

A silence descended for several moments before Deanna finally broke it.

"So let me see if I have this right. You and the ship aren't interested in tourists, you want serious people who want to help. You see your job as something worthy of doing, am I right?"

Arthur shrugged. "Of course. If you had a chance to make sure the world and everyone on it wasn't destroyed, wouldn't you take it seriously? Sounds like a great way to be helpful to me."

"I agree," said Deanna. "Well, I can't speak for anyone else around this table, but I'm willing to help. This sounds like something worthy of doing. I admire your dedication to have done this for so long."

"Count me in. I feel the same way," said Spider, as Clifford nodded vigorously. Everyone else around the table signalled their agreement, too.

This time it was Arthur's turn to be silent for a moment as he considered his response.

"All right, so I've found a whole bunch of people who would like to be helpful and replace me. Do you all truly feel you understand the kind of commitment needed? I mean, do you not all have lives you are leading here, with people and things you are connected to that you could lose if you end up on the saucer? This is a lot to sacrifice."

This time it was Nyota who spoke up after another long silence while everyone considered Arthur's questions.

"Well, we do have lives here and connections to others. But the thing is, our lives are really kind of dull. Look at me. I spent a lot of time in school to end up as a management trainee in a restaurant. Keiko, Harlan, and Jordi all have jobs staring at computer screens all day and if someone were to offer them an opportunity to do something new and different I'm quite certain they would all jump at it. Spider and Clifford, well, these two were already desperate for an opportunity like this to come along. They probably both think they've won the lottery. As it stands, I think everyone will agree the only one of us who actually likes their life and their work is Deanna."

"She's right, Arthur," said Spider. "Our lives, to varying degrees, are all more or less totally boring and mundane. I'm certain we will all jump at the opportunity too. Even Deanna."

"That would be true," said Deanna with a smile. "I really do like to be helpful and I already have opportunities to do that. But a chance to take your place and help on a massive scale like this sounds far more appealing than what I already do."

"Bottom line, I think you actually have a crowd of volunteers, Arthur," said Harlan. "And I know I've been waffling on this, but I think it safe to say you can count me as one of the crowd that would like to help. So I don't know what you want to do about that."

"Hmm. Well, I'm going to have to think about this and somehow explain it all to the ship," said Arthur.

"Arthur?" said Keiko. "For the record, I am sold on the idea too. But what about the possibility of all of us doing it? You said there was plenty of room on the ship. Or maybe we take turns doing it for a bit at a time. I think we would all be flexible."

Arthur scratched his head and sat back in his chair. "I don't know. I never considered any of this as a possibility. I will definitely have to consult the ship on the idea."

"A question for you?" said Harlan. "Once you are certain you've found the right someone, what would happen? How would this work? Would the alien show up to make sure you've got the right person? If so, maybe you could present all of us and see what happens? That is, if you are convinced we are all suitable."

Arthur smiled. "Well, yes, I think I'm convinced you all could work. You are all very different people, but I'm not surprised you are all friends.

You all have more in common than you perhaps realize. Anyway, I don't know what would happen. The alien might show up, you never know."

"Okay, so if we could all be suitable, what is the next step?"

"I push a button."

"A button?" said Clifford. "You mean, a real button? You don't just 'think' a message and pass it on?"

"Nope, I have a real button. Don't have many of those on the ship, but in this case I assure you it's real. I don't know why, but the ship brought it to my attention when this search for a replacement started. Maybe it simply wants to impress on me how important this is? I don't know. It actually has a little cover over it in case I inadvertently push it. I have to take it off before I go to push it. Probably so I don't waste the alien's time by mistake, I guess."

"And you have no idea what will happen or how long it may take for the alien to respond?" said Nyota.

"Nope. But I guess there is only one way to find out. Can you all meet me here for lunch tomorrow?"

On seeing everyone nod, Arthur smiled.

"I don't know if I'll have any kind of a response by then, but we shall find out. See you all tomorrow. I'm off to push a button."

As Arthur vanished from sight Harlan looked around the table at his friends and sighed.

"Hmm. This could be interesting. Well, everyone, good luck sleeping tonight."

Chapter Fourteen

They all showed up at the same time once again, ten minutes early this time, meeting at the entrance to The Lamp. Harlan was unsurprised to find several of them looked a little groggy from having slept poorly. A few of his friends confessed to having taken the morning off as vacation.

Harlan was a little taken aback to find Arthur was already waiting for them, his usual glass of water sitting untouched on the table in front of him. Even stranger, Harlan sensed right away the old man was a little preoccupied. After Carrie took their drink orders and disappeared, Harlan looked around before focusing once again on the old man. Harlan could see no obvious reason for Arthur's distracted look, so he asked Arthur if he was all right.

"Hmm?" replied Arthur. "Oh, yes, I am fine. Just a little puzzled is all. I suppose it must show."

"And why would that be? Have you heard from the alien?"

"Well, not directly, I guess. All I've gotten from the ship is a simple message to 'stand by'. It's more than a bit strange, I'm used to getting something clearer than that. In any case, I'm afraid all I can offer all of you right now is only that. We have to 'stand by'."

"So you pushed your button right after you left us yesterday, right?" asked Deanna.

"Yes."

"And all you've gotten since then is this message. Isn't that a bit long to be waiting?"

"Actually, it is. As I said, I usually get a clear

answer one way or another and it's always been much sooner than this. Sorry, folks. We may have to meet another day to get the answers you are looking for. I hope..."

Harlan and his friends were all so focused on Arthur they were all surprised by the sound of a nearby female voice interrupting their conversation.

"I don't think that will be necessary, Arthur. You are Arthur, correct?"

Everyone turned to find an older, grey haired, petite black woman standing beside the table, wearing a smile and a slightly quizzical look on her face at the same time. Standing beside her was a young, tall and gawky, teenage male with acne problems. On seeing Arthur nod, the old woman looked expectantly around the table at the surprised faces greeting her before she finally spoke again.

"I hope no one would mind if we joined you?"

"Umm, yes, of course. Please do," said Harlan. "Here, let me get some more chairs and make some room."

After they all shifted about and the two new arrivals settled in Harlan introduced everyone. Carrie came by and asked if they would like anything. The old lady peered about, saw the glass of water in front of Arthur, and turned to Carrie.

"We'll have what he's having."

"Somehow I'm not surprised. Won't be making much money around here today. Two waters, coming right up."

As Carrie left Harlan spoke up once again.

"I'm afraid you have the better of us, madam. You are?"

"You're vaguely familiar. I've met you before," said Arthur, looking directly at the teenager while wearing a puzzled look on his face.

"Yes, you have met him before," said the old woman. "My name is Beverly and this is my grandson Wesley."

"Hello Arthur," said the teenager. "It's been a long time, at least for you."

"Well?" said Beverly, directing a frown at her grandson. "Come on, you know what you need to do."

The teenager looked sheepish and averted his eyes for a moment before he finally blurted out what his grandmother obviously wanted him to say.

"Look, I'm...sorry, Arthur. Grandma here has made me understand I shouldn't have done this. Or if I was going to do it, I should have resolved this a lot sooner. I really am sorry it has taken so long."

"Okay, let me get this straight, uh...Beverly," said Spider, obviously unable to resist any longer. "You and your grandson are in fact aliens, correct? So how come you don't look like aliens?"

"Oh, that's easy," she replied. "We know we have to appear in forms you can relate to. Our actual physical appearance would likely send you running to either hide or find a weapon, neither of which you need to do because I assure you we mean you no harm. What you see now is the closest approximation to our actual relationship we could manage. I actually am what you would call his grandmother. His parents are off on...hmm, a remote job, and I am caring for him while they are away. The problem is I haven't been paying enough attention, although that is going to change."

"Fair enough," said Harlan. "But what does 'I shouldn't have done this' mean?"

The teenager squirmed in his seat once again as his grandmother turned to glare at him again.

"Come on, tell them. If you don't, I will."

"Well, I'm still in school, you see? And I was given a project which involved doing a report. I'm supposed to study a developing civilization, provide some analysis, and present some conclusions about whether or not I think the civilization will ultimately succeed, along with my rationale. The thing is I'm a little behind on getting my report done."

"A little?" said his grandmother, giving him a disbelieving look. "How about a lot? Your teacher isn't happy with you."

This time Wesley grimaced before responding.

"Yeah, I know. He chewed me out yesterday. But I told him I needed more time, grandma!"

"Why?"

"This is a weird species, grandma. I learned right away they can be most unpredictable sometimes. And they have a strange attitude toward each other. They don't all seem to regard each other as part of the same species and they fight each other all the time."

"Well, I can't disagree with you on that. It's a fair observation," said Harlan, his face crinkled in puzzlement. "But what does that have to do with anything? Why did you need Arthur here? Did you really want him to stop us from blowing ourselves up?"

"Of course. If you blew yourselves up, what would I do for a report? My teacher would kill me."

Nyota groaned. "So what you're saying is if we blew ourselves up before you could do your report, it would be like having to tell your teacher your dog ate your homework. Or having to explain to him you dropped the ant farm you were studying and broke it before you were done."

"None of that matters now," said Grandma. "Time's up. Your teacher says he thinks you have plenty of information and I agree. And don't give me any more back talk about it, either. I'm not listening."

"So, let me get this straight," said Jordi, wearing the same puzzled look on his face as Harlan. "You say you're appearing to us in forms that reflect your relationship, right? You kidnapped Arthur here decades ago, but you're still a teenager? How old does that make your Grandma? I don't understand."

Beverly smiled. "You are right to be puzzled. Yes, we do age, but our lifespans are much longer than yours. Hmm, let me think. From what I've come to know about you in the short time since I found out about this, I'd say we live roughly fifty of your years for each one that you do. So, yes, Wesley here really is still a teenager, at least from my perspective."

"Okay, I get that," said Keiko. "But I still don't get why you needed to have Arthur around. I understand you didn't want us to blow ourselves up, but why couldn't you just have this super ship that can do all sorts of stuff monitor us and do what was needed to stop us if necessary?"

Wesley shrugged. "Well, you are a very unpredictable and violent species. I figured it would be better to have one of your own to help out, you see? My idea was he might pick up on some subtle piece of information that the ship could easily miss. Who better than a human to watch the humans?"

"Which is another reason why I am not happy with you," said his Grandma, glaring at him once again. "Arthur and his wife have ended up living this abnormal life for a long time on one of our spaceships. I still think you could have done this differently."

"My wife and I haven't minded," said Arthur. "I grant you it's been different, but we've managed all right. We like to be helpful."

"And he was great," said Wesley, a pleading tone in his voice. "It took me a while to find the right person, but when I did I knew he would be fine. Arthur and his wife were perfect and still are. I agree that I've dawdled a bit, but you can see he's doing okay."

"Well, it's ending now, whether you like it or not. I can't change what has happened, but I can give Arthur and his wife their life back. We'll sort that out later, Arthur."

"Good Lord," said Jordi, looking around at his friends. "I'm still having trouble processing this. I mean, what this boils down to is we are all just some high school science project. A bug farm or something, like Nyota said. Anyone else out there questioning the meaning of life, here?"

Beverly looked shocked for a moment and then laughed.

"Oh, no, no. You may be a developing species, but this is no reason to question your value. And there is plenty of meaning in life everywhere. Your species is no different."

"Exactly," said Wesley. "I've never thought of you as bugs. Maybe hamsters, I suppose, or something a little bit more sophisticated. I..."

"Wesley!" barked his grandmother, shaking her head. After glaring at him for a long moment to ensure he stayed silent, she turned back to look at the others and sighed.

"He's still a work in progress, as you can see."

"If I may?" said Arthur, with a mild tone to his voice. "Harlan, I really think you and your friends don't give yourselves enough credit. I was impressed by all of you. I'd say each of you simply need to find a worthy purpose, however small or big it may be, and make it happen. Don't lose your dreams."

"Well said, Arthur," said Beverly.

"So, where does this go from here?" said Keiko.

"They are going to disappear along with Arthur is what will happen," said Deanna. "Beverly and her grandson are holograms, just like Arthur."

"You're very perceptive," said Beverly, looking closer at Deanna. "I'm impressed. You see, there is hope for your species after all. Anyway, I and my wayward grandson are sorry you all became involved. We'll be going now and, rest assured, I will take care of Arthur and his wife."

"Hang on," said Spider. "Aren't you going to do something about us?"

Beverly's face crinkled in puzzlement. "What did

you have in mind?"

An incredulous look came over Spider's face and he gave a sidelong glance at Clifford to see his reaction. Clifford stared back and shrugged, looking equally puzzled.

"Well," said Spider, turning back to Beverly. "Isn't this where you do something to mess with our memories? You know, make us forget ever having met you. We wake up and think we've been probed by aliens or something?"

Beverly chuckled. "Heavens, no. Oh, I suppose we could do that, but I don't know why. I mean, who is going to believe you about any of this?"

"Uh, well, if nothing else we do have these government spooks following us around who seem to believe it."

"Right, the ship told us about them. They aren't a problem. They'll get tired soon enough following you around without Arthur being present. I suppose we could blank their minds if you really want us to?"

Harlan looked around the table as his friends all more or less shrugged at the notion.

"I don't think you need worry about that. You are right, they will lose interest soon enough."

"Actually, they are on the way here again," said Wesley. "I took the liberty of slowing them down so we could have our conversation."

"What does 'slowing them down' mean?" said Harlan. "Nothing permanent, I hope."

"Oh no, the agents themselves are fine. Their van maybe less so," said Wesley with a grin.

Beverly groaned and shook her head.

"Teenagers, I ask you. Come on, let's go. Goodbye, everyone!"

Beverly, Wesley, and Arthur all disappeared in an eyeblink, leaving Harlan and his friends alone at the table. A few of them peered about, as if they might unexpectedly reappear, but the only person who did arrive was Carrie. She wore an incredulous look on her face.

"So, did I actually see that? Those people just disappeared. What is going on here?"

Harlan gave her a pitying look as he replied, pointing behind her.

"We can explain, Carrie, but I'm afraid that will have to wait until after these guys leave."

Everyone turned to see Larry and Ray storm into The Lamp in a rush, their faces reflecting a mixture of anger and frustration. They stalked over to the table and stopped in front of Harlan.

"Okay how did you do that? I want to know, right now, damn it," said Ray.

"Uh, do what, exactly?" said Harlan.

"Come on, don't bullshit us," said Larry. "You know what we are talking about. And while we are at it, who were those two new people with you? The little old lady and the kid."

"Well, the lady was named Beverly and the teenager was Wesley. Beverly is his grandmother. I'm afraid that's the best we can offer, gentlemen. We don't know much more. And I'm sorry, I really don't know what else you may be talking about."

Larry rolled his eyes and took a deep breath.

"Right, let's try this again. I'll make you a deal. I'll do my best to keep my patience while you just please tell me everything you know. Can we do that?"

Harlan shrugged. "We can try. At this point we have no interest in making your life complicated anymore."

"I see," said Larry. "Not sure what that means, but let's keep it simple and start with our van. You can see we are unhappy. What do you know about why?"

"Hmm. Well, I assure you my friends and I had nothing to do with whatever is going on with it. It was the teenager who said he slowed you down. He didn't say how."

"The teenager. Not the old man?"

"Nope. Arthur was not involved with that. It was Wesley."

"Arthur. Well, at least we are getting somewhere with names. But that's it?"

Harlan held his hands open, trying to demonstrate he was hiding nothing.

"You know what we know now."

Larry looked at Ray, who shrugged before both men turned back to Harlan.

"So what would you say if I told you our van is now stuck to the pavement two blocks from here?" said Larry.

"Stuck to the pavement?" said Harlan, a puzzled look appearing on his face. He looked about and saw the same was on the faces of his friends, before turning back to the two agents who were both eyeing them with hard, appraising looks.

"What does that mean?" said Harlan.

Ray finally groaned before speaking. "It means

exactly that. Well, to be more precise, all four tires on our van are flat and have melted to the pavement. We were just driving along and all of a sudden we rolled to a stop. When we checked that is what we found."

"Wow," said Spider. "Did a little green man with a ray gun appear out of nowhere and blast you?"

Ray scowled at Spider in response. "You are such an asshole. I'm going to make a point of finding as much dirt as possible on you."

"Gentlemen, please, no need for that," said Harlan. "As I said, we have nothing to do with that and this is news to us."

Larry sighed. "You know what, Ray? I think I believe them, at least on this point. I can spot a guilty look miles away, and none of them were showing anything even close. So let's move on, shall we? Tell us more about this woman and the kid."

Harlan sighed. "Okay, here it is. I promise, this is the honest to God truth. Beverly and Wesley are both aliens, but Arthur is not. He is human like the rest of us. The teenager kidnapped Arthur and his wife and set them up in a flying saucer to watch over us while he did research for a school project involving the study of humans. Arthur's job was to make sure we didn't blow ourselves up before the kid finished. The problem is the teenager was dawdling. The aliens live much longer lives than us, which is maybe why he was taking his time. Anyway, his teacher and his grandmother, who is his guardian, found out and now he has to get the job done. So Beverly is going to give Arthur and his wife back their life somehow, which I think means you won't be seeing Arthur or their flying saucer anymore. And that's pretty much it."

A profound silence descended on the group as the two blank faced agents remained staring at Harlan, obviously processing what he told them. After close to a minute the two agents turned to look at each other, their faces still blank masks. Ray finally shrugged and held up an empty hand to signal he had nothing to say. Larry scratched his head as he spoke.

"You know, I'm also pretty good at figuring out when someone is bullshitting me. But, God help me, I don't think he is."

"I got nothing," said Ray.

Larry turned to Harlan and sighed.

"You do realize that sounds like a total crock of shit, right? What, are you a science fiction writer, making shit up or something?"

"He isn't, but I am," said Spider. "And I assure you, even in my wildest dreams I couldn't make up bizarre stuff like this. Mind you, this material could be useful. Plenty to work with. You never know, this could be my big break. I can even see the title in my mind. I'll call it The Space Farmer. Hollywood here I come. Well, maybe it'll end up as a B movie, but I'll take it. I've never pretended to be that good a writer and I have no problem being second best if it makes me rich."

"Really, gentlemen, I am serious," said Harlan. "I'll be going home tonight to have a look with my telescope, but I honestly don't think I'll find my anomaly out there anymore and neither will you."

"Nothing to see here, eh?" said Larry.

"Exactly. Nothing at all. Been nice chatting with you fellows."

Another silence descended for a few moments before the two agents looked at each other as one. Larry nodded toward the door, but as he turned to leave he spoke over his shoulder one last time.

"We be seeing you around."

As the door closed behind them Harlan smiled and turned to his friends.

"Somehow I don't think so."

Carrie appeared beside him as he finished speaking and everyone looked up at her. She wore a quizzical look on her face as she spoke to Harlan.

"Sorry. I couldn't help listening in because I was curious. Was all that stuff you said true?"

Harlan nodded. "I'm afraid so."

"So we're, like, an ant farm for aliens? Or maybe pet hamsters, like the kid said?"

"Well, I think we really are more than that, but how much more? I honestly don't know."

"Huh. Well, this all sounds like a good reason to drink more beer. Who wants some?"

Epilogue

The flight attendant came by to pick up the now empty coffee cup, distracting Harlan from staring out the window at the broad sweep of open farmland steadily passing by below. The pilot began their descent ten minutes before and the aircraft was now low enough Harlan could easily make out neatly sectioned parcels of land, each with its own colour depending on the crop being grown. He could see cattle in some of the sections in the fields, while others had only the tiny figure of a lone farmer on his tractor. Watching the scene passing below helped Harlan to lose track of how many times the question bubbled to the surface of his mind of what he would find at his destination. He knew he was still without an answer, but soon, though, he was optimistic he would.

The desire to know was impossible to resist, after having first appeared in his mind late in the evening of the day Arthur and the other aliens disappeared. As expected, when he trained his telescope on the coordinates where Arthur's flying saucer was located the anomaly was no longer there. The government agents with their mysterious van continued to follow him around for a week afterwards, but Harlan simply ignored them and soon enough he no longer saw any sign of them. With the anomaly gone and no reason to carry on, he was certain they were giving up.

Although they were gone as expected, Harlan's curiosity remained and now, two weeks later, he was about to land and find out whether he could indeed learn more about Arthur and the aliens. A search of the internet to locate a farm near Vulcan owned by a couple named Arthur and Ursula didn't take long to complete, and it quickly bore fruit.

Unable to resist, Harlan booked a ticket on the less than two-hour flight to the city closest to the farm. The car he rented at the airport came with onboard navigation, so it was easy to carry on the rest of the way. He drove into the city and checked into his hotel, intending to set out for the farm right after breakfast.

Soon enough the next morning he was free of the heavy traffic of the city and driving the highway through the gently rolling, flat Prairie fields, which sped by during the hour-long drive to where he was going. Occasionally, dilapidated old grain elevators worn by the elements were easily visible in the distance, appearing alongside newer ones in some of the smaller towns he drove past.

Eventually the navigation told him to turn off the main highway onto a series of narrow, gravel country roads a little over an hour later. After enduring the bumpy, dusty ride of the gravel side roads, Harlan finally found himself at the entrance to an even smaller branch leading to a nearby farmhouse.

Harlan drove up and parked in front. No one was about or came out to greet him, so he went to the front door and knocked. After a minute the door opened and an older, white-haired woman peered out at him, a quizzical look on her face.

"Hello? Can I help you?" she said.

"Umm, hello. My name is Harlan. I'm looking

for a friend. His name is Arthur. He told me his wife's name was Ursula. By any chance would that be you?"

"Well, yes. I guess you've come to the right place. I sorry, I confess I don't know you. How do you know Arthur?"

Harlan was wary right away, surprised that she wouldn't know his name. He told her where he was from and that he recalled meeting Arthur while travelling. This time she looked bemused.

"Travelling? Arthur and I haven't done much in the way of travelling. In fact, I know for certain he's never been close to where you're from. No matter, if he's met you before I'm sure he will remember you. Come on in, I think he's out in the field at the back."

Harlan waited in the living room while Ursula went to find Arthur. A moment later she came back and gestured for him to join her. She pointed out the back door of the house.

"He's over there. Looks like he's working on the fence. Why don't you just walk over and say hello?"

"Sure, thank you."

Harlan made his way out the back yard and into the field, which he quickly realized was a field of wheat almost ready for harvest. A pleasant breeze made the wheat ripple like it was the surface of a pond. A few minutes later Harlan drew close to where Arthur was working.

Arthur appeared to see Harlan from the corner of his eye and stood up to greet him. With relief Harlan realized it was indeed Arthur, but his sense of succeeding quickly disappeared on seeing the blank look on Arthur's face. After introducing himself and shaking hands once again, Harlan asked if Arthur really didn't remember him.

"Sorry, son, you aren't familiar at all. You say I apparently met you travelling? I don't know where or when that would have been. My wife and I don't get out much, you see. We've spent all our lives here and I've never cared much for the big city, which we've never been beyond. Too much noise and traffic. I've gone there to buy some equipment a few times. Maybe that's when I met you?"

"Uh, could have been Arthur. It was only a passing meeting a long time ago. A friend of a friend introduced us. Yeah, it was in a store, come to think of it. Anyway, I was in the neighbourhood and thought I would stop by to say hello, see if you remembered me. We enjoyed a good chat that day. I shouldn't have intruded. Well, look, it is nice to see you and meet Ursula. I should be on my way."

As he turned to go Arthur waved at him to stop.

"Nonsense, you are here now. Just because my memory is going after all these years is no reason for you to leave. You should stay for lunch. We're having Greek food today, I think. Come on, let's go in and see."

"Hmm, you could be right, Arthur. It would have been hard to miss the smell of garlic as I went through the kitchen."

Back at the house Ursula peered expectantly at Arthur, who shrugged in response.

"I must be older than I thought, my love. Harlan here says we met in the city a long time ago and had a good talk, but I'm darned if I remember any of it. He's here now, though, and I took the liberty of inviting him to stay for lunch."

Arthur grinned and looked at Harlan before continuing.

"I didn't need to ask her if it was okay. She always makes extra in case this kind of situation happens. People drop by to visit all the time around here. By the way, there actually is one thing I should have asked of you. I hope you like Greek food?"

"I love it, Arthur. I'd eat Greek food every day if I could."

"We both love Greek food," said Ursula. "In fact, we like all kinds of different foods from all over the world. Isn't that the strangest thing? Here we've never travelled more than a couple of hundred miles from here all our lives, but we like food from all these different places. Asian food, you name it. We even like sushi, but we have to drive into town for that."

"Yes, it's a bit odd, isn't it?" said Arthur. "But Ursula here is a great cook and she makes the best chicken and prawn souvlaki anywhere. I expect the only place it would be better is in Greece."

"Funny you mention this, Arthur," said Harlan with a smile. "I have a memory of you telling me how much you both like Greek food. Thank you both for the offer of lunch. You know, you struck me as a real nice guy when we met and I see that hasn't changed. And I have to say, I am very, very glad to see you are both doing well."

***

Harlan made his way out to his patio with a beer in hand, taking a long pull at it before sitting down in a chair and putting his beer on the table. The late summer night was warm and pleasant, with skies clear enough even a few stars could be seen despite the lights of the city. Harlan found himself tempted to get out his telescope once again, but somehow after everything that happened he knew it was most unlikely he would ever find himself in another situation like this. But as he got comfortable and made to reach for his glass again, a familiar presence appeared beside him.

"Meow!" said Spock. As Harlan looked down at the cat he realized it was as if Harlan no longer mattered, now that Spock was getting the attention he deserved. The cat was now giving his full attention to licking a paw. Harlan laughed.

"Oh, I get it, you greedy little bugger. You're just waiting for a treat, aren't you?"

The cat paused for the briefest of moments to eye Harlan, before going right back to what he was doing.

"I swear, you think I'm dense, don't you?" said Harlan, rising from his chair to find a bag of cat treats. "And who knows, maybe you're right."

As Harlan returned and began feeding treats to the now very attentive cat another familiar voice came from next door.

"Is he over there bothering you again?" said Isaac. "Sorry, he hasn't seen you for a while."

"Not a problem, Isaac. Why don't you bring a drink and join us?"

A minute later Isaac came over and sat down, his own glass of beer in hand.

"Good to see you again," said Isaac. "It has been

a while. Spock and I were away travelling for a bit, and then you left yourself. Were you away on business?"

"No, actually. I've got a bit of a story to tell and it's all about my space farmer, if you can believe it."

"Really? This sounds interesting."

"It is. I..." said Harlan, pausing as his phone rang to let him know someone was at his door. Harlan rose from his seat to let them in, while calling over his shoulder. "Hang on a minute, Isaac."

A couple of minutes later Harlan brought Keiko out to the patio, after stopping in the kitchen to get her a glass of wine. As soon as Harlan finished making introductions and she was comfortably seated, Spock appeared beside her.

"Oh, what a lovely cat! I didn't know you had one, Harlan."

"Actually, he belongs to me," said Isaac. "But he does spend half his time over here with Harlan."

Spock gave another meow and promptly jumped into Keiko's lap, settling down in seconds. Isaac laughed.

"Spock likes the ladies."

"Spock?" said Keiko, a wary look on her face. "Another science fiction fan? Somehow it doesn't surprise me you would be Harlan's neighbour."

"Strictly coincidence, I assure you. So, you have more of the story to tell about your space farmer, Harlan?"

"That's the reason I'm here," said Keiko. "I'm curious to know if he found Arthur."

"I have to go back a little further before I get to that, Keiko," said Harlan. "Isaac here has been travelling too, and he hasn't heard what happened when the aliens showed up."

"The aliens finally made an appearance, did they? Well, this will be interesting. Please proceed, I'm all ears."

Harlan spent the next ten minutes telling Isaac what happened with Wesley and his grandmother, before finishing the story with details of his trip to find Arthur and his wife. Isaac laughed when he learned the reason behind Arthur being selected to watch over humanity.

"Have to say I didn't see that one coming. Most amusing. Nice to see they took care of Arthur and his wife, though."

"It is," said Keiko, a thoughtful look on her face. "But I wonder why the aliens erased their memory and not ours?"

"Hmm, it may have to do with reversing the effects of the physiological changes the aliens made to Arthur and his wife in order to give them much longer lives. I suspect living on the ship may have prolonged matters. Once they moved off the ship permanently, I'll bet their lives would have rapidly ended. So the aliens reversed the changes and gave them back a golden retirement to age naturally."

Harlan and Keiko both looked at each other for a long moment, before turning back to Isaac.

"I say," said Harlan. "That seems like a rather perceptive notion. Don't think I would have thought of that."

"Same for me," said Keiko.

Isaac laughed. "I guess it takes one to know one."

Harlan and Keiko quickly looked at each other from the corner of their eyes before turning back to Isaac.

"Uh," said Keiko. "And that means?"

"I'm an alien, too, of course," said Isaac with a grin. "I normally don't confess that to anybody, but since I'm leaving it doesn't matter much. And I have to say I've thoroughly enjoyed spending time talking to you, Harlan."

"I see," said Harlan. "And you are indeed leaving? Where are you off to? Returning to your home world?"

Isaac chuckled. "No, not yet. I'm off to a place you wouldn't be familiar with and no, I'm not heading anywhere else on your planet, if that is what you are wondering. I believe I told you I sort of do diplomatic work, right? Well, my part time job in my retirement is to take the time to check out new worlds and species, sort out whether it's time to reveal ourselves to them or not. I won't be running out of work any time soon. Anyway, sorry to say humans aren't quite ready for that yet, but I'm optimistic a day will come when you are."

"Fascinating," said Keiko. "But there's one thing I don't get. How come you don't seem to have known anything about the aliens that kidnapped Arthur?"

"Oh, they are a totally different species from my people. We do have relations with them, but that's about it."

"Okay, so the aliens that kidnapped Arthur hinted at the same thing, that humans aren't ready for prime time, so to speak. Out of curiosity, what is it humans have failed at?"

"Dealing with each other, of course. Your species is really very aggressive when you want to be, which is far too often for our tastes. The civilized universe out there won't tolerate such behaviour. We have the equivalent of your United Nations as an entity to work with each other and in our case it works far better than your version. As a part of our work together we explore and look for new worlds and civilizations, which is what I do."

"Wow," said Keiko. "Somehow I think I know the answer to this, but what would happen if we developed to a point where we learned about your existence, but we hadn't lost our aggressive tendencies?"

Isaac grimaced. "Sorry, but it's likely we would have to turn the clock back on you a bit. You know, two steps forward and one back. The Dark Ages didn't just happen by themselves, right? But on the plus side, we've also stopped you from wiping yourselves out, too. Humans have a lot greater history than you realize."

"Wow," said Harlan. "So, let's see if I have this straight. The aliens that kidnapped Arthur figure we're little better than a teenager's science experiment. Meanwhile, you and your species see us as still in the little leagues and likely to be there for a very long time."

"True, but don't get the impression you are without value. I've told my superiors you have plenty of potential. Capable of surprise in both good and bad ways is what my report said. I know, you are wondering at the meaning of it all and maybe even you were thinking the universe is meaningless. But please do think again. Anyway, Spock and I must be off. I really have enjoyed my time here, Harlan. Who knows, I may even pop back to see you one day."

As he finished speaking Spock jumped down from Keiko's lap and onto Isaac's. As Spock settled down once again he grinned at Harlan and Keiko.

"Thanks for all the treats, Harlan," said Spock. "I don't know how you humans do it, but the treats on my world just aren't as good as the ones you have. Goodbye!"

The moment he finished speaking both Isaac and Spock winked out of sight, exactly like Arthur and the other aliens. The only difference was Spock somehow contrived to have a brief image of only his grin linger for a second in the air before it too disappeared.

Harlan and Keiko both sat there staring at the now empty space occupied by the two aliens only moments before. They both remained silent for a long time, before finally turning to look at each other. Another moment passed before Keiko spoke.

"God Almighty, how do you do this, Harlan?"

"Uh, do what?"

"Attract aliens. Like, is there anything else I need to know? Got any hiding under your bed? Or in your closet? Come to think of it, how do I know you aren't some alien?"

Harlan shrugged and laughed. "I have no idea why me and I have none hiding anywhere. Last I checked, I'm as human as I believe you are."

Keiko was silent once again as she stared at him,

a contemplative appearance to her face, which slowly changed to an apologetic look.

"Harlan? I'm sorry. I really am."

"Sorry? For what?"

"For having doubted you. I think I've come to understand you aren't the nerdy dweeb I thought you were. Well, science geek may still be applicable, but no, I no longer think you're some kind of a loser."

Harlan laughed. "I'm glad. This is who I am. I can live with being a geek if you can accept me as that. We all search to find who we really are. Maybe we've been searching for each other, too?"

Keiko hesitated for a brief moment before reaching out her hand to let Harlan take it in his own.

"Hard to believe what I've been searching for has been here in front of me all along, and I've been too blind to see it. So let's see what the future holds, Harlan."

The End

Author Notes

I have a couple of apologies to offer.

First, and most important, I do hope no one reading this book thought it was going to be a serious work of science fiction, or of any other kind of fiction for that matter. There is nothing at all serious in this other than a desire to provide some light entertainment to anyone choosing to read it.

Strange as this may seem, I'm not entirely sure where the concept for this came from, although I have some ideas. I suspect it is a blend of a variety of inspirational sources, not the least of which is the influence of every other book or movie I've ever read or seen. But for whatever reason, I recall feeling the need to work on something more light-hearted, like it was time 'for something completely different', if all the comedy fans reading this know what I mean. I probably don't even have to wink or nudge you to make sure you get the joke.

The fact is I'm writing these words in 2022 and I suspect there are plenty of people out there who would share the thought we've had more than enough serious stuff going on in the world the last few years. Maybe it's because I'm a senior citizen these days. I'd rather laugh and enjoy myself than read some dark novel with a lot of angst and bad happenings in it.

So I think along with that need on my part came the memory I used to enjoy science fiction a lot when I was much younger and, as it happens, I read plenty of it back then. Those of you who enjoy this genre will likely have noticed all of the characters in this book have names associated with science fiction books and tv shows. Spock is the easiest one to notice, of course. Seriously, could there be any consumer of entertainment on this planet that doesn't get that reference?

The others vary in degree of obscurity, but I won't keep you in suspense in case any of you haven't figured them out. For starters there are a bunch of characters from various tv series, all involving wagon trains to the stars in one form or another (Nyota, Wesley, Keiko, Jordi, Deanna, Beverly). And, yes, in case you actually need me to state the obvious, I confess I am indeed a Trekkie.

A few of my favourite science fiction writers are also the inspiration for other character names in this book (Arthur C. Clarke, Isaac Asimov, Spider Robinson, Ursula K. LeGuin, Ray Bradbury, Larry Niven, Harlan Ellison, Robert Heinlein, Clifford Simak). For those of you who didn't go through a science fiction phase like me, I do endorse all of these writers and I could easily recommend more. Some of their work is what I call hard science fiction, with a focus on the real technical aspects of space science, while there are large elements of fantasy in the others. Brilliant stuff, some of it more offbeat than others, but all of it well worth the read.

Anyway, despite not knowing exactly where the notion came from that I should try my hand at a hybrid fantasy science fiction book, when it did appear in my head I felt a need to do a homage to my somewhat misspent youth reading a ton of it. All the character name references are therefore here as my small token of appreciation for the creators behind all of these wonderful stories.

I'd say one remaining piece of the puzzle was needed, though, to make this book happen. I believe it was around the same time all this was percolating in my mind that the American military finally got around to confessing they really have had numerous encounters with flying objects they cannot identify or explain.

Somehow, I think, all this clanged together in my head and I thought to myself "Well, *of course* I can explain why aliens were abducting people back in the nineteen fifties. No problem".

A bit of a daunting task perhaps, but I was never afraid to grab a shovel and start spreading the horse manure around if it would get me through an assignment in school or university. A few of my teachers and professors noticed, too. Anyway, that brewed in my head for a while and now here you have it, nothing serious to see here.

The other apology I must make, however, is to all the SETI researchers and space scientists out there. Science geeks they certainly are, but to me that is a good and worthy thing to be. Science was never my forte, but I have great appreciation for scientists everywhere. The world would be a far less pleasant place without them. I know, sometimes scientists develop stuff we'd rather they didn't, but that isn't the fault of the science. Anyway, I only want to be clear I mean no disrespect to all the hard-working scientists out there striving to make this a better world.

And, yes, I do believe there are aliens out there and I think the SETI people will succeed one day.

Rather presumptuous of us to assume there aren't aliens out there, don't you think? I suspect a few other species are somewhere in some obscure part of the universe similar to our own thinking the same thing, and maybe there are even more that are busy actually watching us.

If so, let's hope they decide we are worth getting to know better and don't blast us back to the Dark Ages because they see us as a threat. It might be a good idea on our part to make ourselves worthy enough to be their friends and ensure they don't reach for their ray guns.

One small side note, as you may or may not know about this. There actually is a small town on the Canadian Prairies called Vulcan and they did indeed build a quite large replica of a rather well-known spaceship back in 1995, which is still there today. Do an internet search using 'Vulcan Alberta spaceship' as the search terms and you will see.

So now I'm done with my completely silly, different project and I'm going back to writing historical fiction, which I've been doing for a while now. If you enjoy that genre, you have more interesting stories on your horizon. The entire era from the beginning of the American Revolution through to the Battle of Trafalgar is fascinating and the Caribbean was in the thick of many of the tumultuous events of the time.

If you have interest, please do take a look at the six books in The Evan Ross Series if you haven't already done so. You can find details on my website lylegarford.com or on Amazon and other retailers. In series order, they are:

Dockyard Dog
The Sugar Revolution
The Sugar Sacrifice
The Sugar Rebellion
The Sugar Inferno
The Admiral's Pursuit

You can also look forward to The Owen Spence Series. This will eventually consist of a total of three works, in the following order:

The Sugar Sands
The Sugar Storm
The Sugar Winds

The Sugar Storm is my next project and will take you to a couple of small Caribbean islands most readers likely know little about, if you have even heard of them before. The first of these is St. Eustatius, which in our times has lapsed into obscurity, but for a few brief years in the late 1770's it was quite the opposite.

You will also visit the little-known island of Dominica and enjoy its rich history in *The Sugar Storm*. For those of you who may not know, the fascinating island of Dominica is not to be confused with The Dominican Republic, a popular vacation destination with plenty of all-inclusive beach resorts occupying half of the nearby island of Hispaniola.

Both St. Eustatius and Dominica were very much worthy of the attention of the world powers involved in the Caribbean in this era. To find out why, watch for *The Sugar Storm*, coming in 2023.

I hope you have enjoyed *The Space Farmer*. And I do hope I managed to get at least one smile or perhaps even a laugh or two out of you while you read this.

The world needs more of both.